HAUNTED CHRISTMAS
GHOST STORIES

Jo-Anne Christensen

GHOST HOUSE

Ghost House Books

The Publisher: Ghost House Books
Distributed by Lone Pine Publishing
10145 – 81 Avenue
Edmonton, AB T6E 1W9
Canada
Website: http://www.ghostbooks.net

National Library of Canada Cataloguing in Publication Data
Christensen, Jo-Anne
    Haunted Christmas

    ISBN 1-894877-15-2

    1. Ghosts. 2. Christmas. I. Title.
BF1471.C47 2002   398.23'6   C2002-910899-3

Editorial Director: Nancy Foulds
Project Editor: Shelagh Kubish
Production Coordinator: Jennifer Fafard
Book Design, Layout & Production: Ian Dawe
Illustrations: Ian Dawe
Cover Design: Gerry Dotto & Elliot Engley

We acknowledge the financial support of the Government of Canada through the Book Publishing Industry Development Program (BPIDP) for our publishing activities.

PC: P5

Dedication

For Auntie Joan and my cousins Tammy and Mark, with whom I have spent many happy Christmases

CONTENTS

Acknowledgments

Every day of my life, I am grateful for the opportunity to earn my living in this way. I am also fully aware that it would not be possible without the support, encouragement and talents of many wonderful people in my professional and personal worlds. Their contributions to my career in general and to this book in particular have been invaluable.

My appreciation goes out first to the staff and management of Ghost House Books. It's a treat to work with such an accomplished and professional group. I thank Shane Kennedy and Nancy Foulds for being as supportive and enthusiastic as always, and Ian Dawe for bringing the stories to life with his marvelous illustrations. Those same stories were made much more clear and strong through the process of Shelagh Kubish's eagle-eye editing. Having Shelagh as an editor is like knowing that the best sharpshooter in the unit has "got your back." Her talents significantly improve everything I write. Working with her, I must add, is a pure pleasure.

My very close friend and fellow author Barbara Smith contributes in ways both concrete and intangible to each project of mine. This time, I dragged her right into the trenches with me when things got ugly. Thank you, Barbara, for the brainstorming, the kick-starting and the vegetarian lasagna. You got me out of the slump.

As always, I owe a debt of gratitude to my family—the foundation of my happy writing house—for their endless support. Thank you to my children, Steven, Grace, William and Natalie, and to my husband, Dennis, who never fails me. I'm proud of you and grateful for you and I love you, always.

Introduction

If ever there is a time to believe in what seems unbeliev-able, it is Christmas. The holiday season is a landscape built of idealistic hopes and dreams—it is a time when the most cynical among us want to believe in things unimag-inable and, sometimes, bordering on the impossible.

We believe that warring factions of our families will get along for the sake of the annual visit. We believe that we can get the Christmas cards out on time, with a per-sonal note tucked into each one. We believe that we can produce home-baked cookies and handmade gifts and create something resembling the glossy, catalog-cover, picture-perfect, family Christmases that we see on televi-sion. And we believe that we can bring it all in on time and under budget.

Given that, is it really so difficult to believe in ghosts?

Someone close to me was once visited by the spirit of her dead son while she mixed the stuffing for the turkey on Christmas morning. I believed her when she told me about it. I believed her because she's an honest person and because there are scores of true ghost stories that take place during the festive season. They are often heart-warming tales of loved ones returning or of generous souls offering comfort to those who need it most. It may be that these spirits, being compassionate, come to us at a time of year when goodwill is traditionally spread. Or it may be that at this innocent time of year when we are willing to believe that "yes, Virginia, there is a Santa Claus," our minds are open to perceive other miraculous things as well.

It's something to think about.

Personally, I have abandoned many of my own yuletide convictions. I no longer believe that I'll manage to have the gifts wrapped before December 24, and I no longer believe that I can spend the month of December surrounded by chocolates and not gain 10 pounds.

But I do believe in ghosts...

And I love a Christmas ghost story...

And I hope that you will, too.

It's the best you'll get from me where the holidays are concerned, because my cards never get out on time.

Part One: Friends

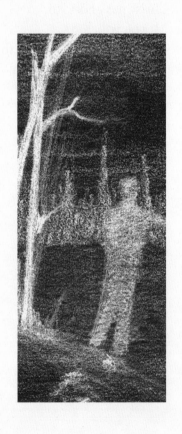

"There are no strangers on Christmas Eve."

—*Beyond Tomorrow* (1940), directed by Edward Sutherland

Spanner's Gift

Owen Piercy was an honest, hard-working man during the Great Depression, when it was not easy to be either of those things. At a time when so many men routinely swallowed their pride or had given it up altogether, Owen would not let go of the notion that there should always be a day's work for a day's pay. The labor was often back-breaking, and the wages were sometimes no more than a bowl of thin soup and a place to lay his head, but Owen never complained. As long as he could say that he had put in an honest day for what little comfort he had, he was happy enough.

The jobs Owen took rarely lasted more than a few days. Frequently, he would find himself riding the rails to a new town, looking for new opportunities. On Christmas Eve of 1933, this was the case. Unfortunately, it was a day better suited to those who were searching for charity. Owen politely thanked everyone who offered him a hand-out but insisted that he was looking for work.

"Try out west of town," one woman finally suggested. "Lots of homesteads out that way. Might be some work, if you're determined to get it."

Owen was determined and he thanked the woman for her suggestion. He found the narrow, rutted road that led west of the small town and set out on foot.

It started out as a good day to be walking. The bare branches of the trees reached up into a brilliant blue sky, and the air was soft and mild for a December day. By the time the sun was lowering itself to the horizon, however, the weather had begun to change. The sky turned steely and the temperature dropped. A frigid north wind swept in ominous, low clouds. Icy snowflakes began to fall. Owen Piercy turned up the frayed collar of his ragged cloth coat and wondered if he shouldn't have made an exception and spent Christmas back in town, in the soup kitchen or the basement of the church.

When darkness fell, the snowfall became heavier, the wind howled more viciously and soon a wicked blizzard was raging. Owen struggled against the storm with every step. His hands and feet grew numb with cold and his face was left raw and stinging by the bitter gusts of wind. What bothered Owen the most, though, what truly frightened him, was that he was barely able to see through the blinding blanket of white. Simply following the main road had come to require all of his concentration. He knew that he would never be able to see a farmhouse set back in the trees or an unmarked drive leading away from the main road.

I'm going to freeze, he finally admitted to himself. *I'm going to freeze to death on this deserted road before Christmas morning comes.*

The grim thought had just taken hold when Owen caught sight of a dark shape in the midst of the swirling white. He wiped the ice from his frozen eyelashes and squinted into the distance. There was a man no more than 30 feet ahead, a bearded man standing in what Owen believed to be the middle of the road.

He was beckoning Owen to follow him.

With a broad gesture, the man pointed to the right. Then he turned and walked away in that direction. Owen couldn't see a path, but he had to trust that one was there. He turned as well and, desperate to not lose sight of the stranger, forced his deadened feet to run a few stumbling steps. There was ice beneath the snow, though, and a steep hill where the path led up to the road. Owen couldn't see it. He slipped and fell hard on the frozen ground.

"Wait! I'm coming!" he shouted through lips that were nearly too frozen to form the words.

The stranger did wait; he must have, for when Owen looked up again, the man was no farther ahead of him than he'd been before. He stood patiently, watching Owen struggle to his feet. Then, as soon as Owen took a step toward him, the bearded man turned and began walking away.

It seemed strange to Owen that the man hadn't waited for him to catch up. Stranger still, he seemed unwilling to *let* him catch up. Even when Owen increased his pace, the stranger managed to maintain a steady distance between them. That he appeared to do so effortlessly, without hurrying himself, had to be a strange illusion created by the storm. It was a curious thing that would have interested Owen had he been in less dire circumstances.

For a good quarter-mile, he followed the stranger down into a thickly forested ravine. Though Owen grew more wretchedly frozen with every step, the other fellow appeared nearly oblivious to the blizzard that wailed around them. He stood straight, not bent against the wind as Owen was, and he never slipped or lost his footing on the treacherous path. What was more, he never hugged himself for warmth or blew into his cupped hands, although he wore nothing more than a pair of sturdy work pants and a long-sleeved shirt. The stranger strode ahead smoothly, easily. In the limited visibility, he appeared to Owen to veritably glide across the snow.

Just as Owen had begun to think that he could not plow through the drifts any farther, the man led him into a little clearing. At the center of it stood a solid-looking log cabin that was nearly invisible between the snow that was banked against its walls and the snow that blew around it in furious, white sheets. The man walked up to the door of the cabin and turned to face Owen. He opened his mouth, creating a round, black pit in the middle of his bushy beard. Although the darkness and the blizzard prevented Owen from seeing the man's lips move, he clearly heard him speak.

"I must go," he said, in a flat British accent, "but you're very welcome here."

There was a sudden gust of wind and snow. Owen covered his eyes to protect them from the stinging blast. A moment later, when he lowered his hands, the stranger had already gone.

Owen squinted into the darkness. He saw no other buildings in the clearing, but then, he reasoned, he could barely see the one that was directly in front of him. The stranger had clearly been in no distress and had obviously known where he was going. To stand there in the freezing cold worrying about the man seemed extremely foolish. Instead, Owen struggled the last few steps through the blizzard and pushed open the cabin's sturdy plank door.

He found himself in a room that seemed so snug and safe that he nearly wept with relief. A kerosene lamp, turned low, sat on a small table made of wooden crates and cast a warm light over its surroundings. A fire in the cast-iron, pot-bellied stove still smoldered, giving off waves of welcoming heat. And, best of all, Owen noted, the chinks in the walls had been tightly packed with clumps of moss and mud. The mixture, which had dried on the logs in ugly gray smears, was doing an efficient job of keeping the warmth in and the weather out. The wailing of the storm was suddenly muted and distant; no freezing evidence of it seemed able to penetrate the sturdy little dwelling.

"Thank you, God," Owen whispered. "Thank you, I'm saved." Then he set about making his new surroundings even more accommodating.

He found a stack of dry wood against one wall and fed the fire in the stove until it was roaring. As the cabin grew warmer, he dared to peel off his coat and unlace his worn, old boots. There was a comfortable chair near the stove, and Owen sat in it. He held his hands and feet in the radiant heat and rubbed his numb fingers and toes vigorously, coaxing the blood to circulate.

Once his body had thawed, Owen felt a twinge of guilt over having built such a large, crackling fire.

"I shouldn't be using all of this fellow's cordwood," he told himself. But, instantly, on the tail of his remorseful thought, came the echo of the stranger's words.

You're very welcome...

It was like having a memory of what the man had said—only it was more vivid and real than a mere memory. It was almost as if Owen had heard the stranger speak again. He marveled at that for a moment and then simply took heed of the message. He understood that he was welcome to the wood and the comfort of the fire. It was a relief to Owen, who felt too weak to do anything other than sit in front of the glowing stove.

He was weak because he hadn't eaten in nearly two days. Nailed to the wall above the woodpile were a few crude pantry shelves, stocked with an assortment of appetizing looking tins and packages. Owen's stomach cramped and groaned at the thought of them.

"Don't think about it," he told himself as he squeezed his eyes shut to keep from looking over at the shelves. He wouldn't allow himself to steal food, no matter how starved he was. As he battled with the insistent hunger pangs, however, the stranger's voice reminded him:

You're very welcome...

Could the man have been talking about the food, too? Owen could barely allow himself to think about it. Finally, because his mouth would not stop watering and his stomach would not stop clenching, he decided that he would help himself to a small meal.

"I can repay him tomorrow," Owen rationalized, to ease his conscience. "There has to be some job I could do around here." With that promise made, he went to the shelves to see what he could find.

He found a feast.

Owen discovered that once he started eating, he could not stop. He opened three tins of oily sardines and ate them spread over pieces of crisp, brown hardtack. He used store-bought cookies like spoons to scoop blackberry jam out of a jar and boiled water in a battered tin pot to make sugary, black tea. He found a bin of potatoes and peeled and cooked two of the largest. When they were tender, he used a blackened fork to mash them with a scoop of bacon drippings and a generous pinch of salt. Finally, when all of that had been consumed, he opened a tin of peaches for his dessert. It wasn't until he was licking the last of the thick, sweet syrup off his fingers that he felt shame setting in.

He had eaten so much, surely more than the man had intended him to take.

"I'll work as long as it takes to pay you back," Owen promised out loud. "There must be some way I can be of use to you."

Owen wanted to be a considerate guest, so he cleaned up the few crumbs that remained of his meal and threw them into the stove. He washed out the pot that he had cooked in and the dented dipper he had drunk from. As he set them back on the shelf, he noticed a handsome, leather-bound Bible that had earlier escaped his attention. He eyed it as hungrily as he had eyed the food the hour before. It would be comforting to read a few verses, especially given that it was Christmas Eve.

"But it's not mine and it wouldn't be right, going through another man's personal belongings," Owen lectured himself.

You're very welcome...

Owen paused, but only for a moment. It seemed that the stranger meant for him to truly make himself at home, so he took the Bible down from the shelf, carried it over to the comfortable chair by the glowing stove and sat down to read.

It wasn't long before Owen began to nod off. It seemed that exhaustion had held off just long enough to allow all his other needs to be met. Owen thought of how wonderful it would feel to stretch his tired, aching body out in a warm bed and decided to retire for the night. He closed the Bible

he had been reading. As he did so, he noticed a blue scrawl of loopy handwriting on the inside of the cover. Although he felt as though he was snooping, he took a look.

John Spanner, it read. And, underneath the name: *Born February 17, 1891.*

"John Spanner," Owen said, as he pictured the tall man with the bushy beard who had led him to safety and comfort. "I guess I know who to thank, come morning." He set the Bible on the table, turned the kerosene lamp down low and yawned.

The cabin consisted of one cozy room, but John Spanner had built a kind of loft at one end of it. A ladder led to a high bunk bed of sorts; it was a small, enclosed space designed to hold in warmth, even as the fire died out and the rest of the cabin grew cool. Owen could see the corners of a thick quilt and a heavy woolen blanket draped over the side of the bed. He started up the ladder, eagerly anticipating the good rest he was about to have.

But, at the top of the ladder, Owen Piercy froze.

There, lying on top of the soft, patchwork cover, was a man. A dead man. The same man who had led Owen to his cabin.

Though it seemed impossible to reconcile those two facts, Owen knew them both to be true. The fellow in the bed was easily recognizable by his bristly whiskers and his coarse, drab work clothing. But he was cold, he was stiff and his pallor was as gray as the shirt he wore. There was no rhythmic rise and fall of his chest, and worse, his eyes, half-lidded, were fixed in a final unfocused gaze.

Owen reached up with a trembling hand and closed John Spanner's staring eyes. Suddenly, he found himself remembering the effortless way the man had been able to glide over the snow and the curious way that the wind had not whipped his shirttails about and the peculiar way that he had spoken, by simply opening his mouth but not really moving it. Owen remembered all of it in a rush and had to carefully climb down the ladder before he swooned and fell.

Once Owen had steadied himself, he retrieved the Bible from the table and found an appropriate passage. He read aloud and said a simple prayer for John Spanner, who lay dead in his comfortable bed. Then, because it was very late and nothing else could be done, Owen wrapped himself in a blanket and settled into the chair by the pot-bellied stove. His last thought before sleep was the unhappy realization that he would never have the opportunity to repay his generous host.

By the next morning—Christmas morning—the storm had passed. Owen ate a small breakfast of tea and porridge, then put on his boots and coat, which had dried nicely by the fire.

"I'll be back, John Spanner," he promised solemnly as he closed the cabin door behind him.

Even though the weather was calm and clear, it took Owen more than an hour to trudge down the road to the nearest farmhouse. He knew for a fact that he never would have made it that far in the blizzard. He would have ended up as dead as Spanner, his corpse left to be ravaged by wild animals. There would have been no dignity in that death, and Owen Piercy was a man who believed in proper endings.

The place he found was large and well kept. As Owen crossed the tidy yard, he noted almost subconsciously that it was the sort of farm where a fellow could usually find a few days' worth of work. But, for once, Owen wasn't interested in a job. There was old work to finish before he could start looking for something new.

The door was answered by a large man whose frowning features told Owen that he didn't like being bothered by a vagrant on Christmas Day.

"I'm here about your neighbor," Owen said quickly, so there would be no misunderstanding.

"Which one?" the man asked, still holding the screen door shut, still wearing a suspicious expression.

"John Spanner, I think his name is. Big fellow with a beard. Got a cabin east of here, down in the gully."

"The Englishman, sure. What about him?"

"Well," Owen spoke carefully, not knowing how close a relationship the neighbors had. "I'm sorry to say he's dead."

"Ah, no, is that so?" The man's face softened, and he opened the screen door. Instead of inviting Owen into the house, however, he joined him out on the veranda. "That's a shame, he was a nice fella," the man said. "Bit of a loner. Hadn't been feeling well since summer, though. Kept saying he meant to see the doctor in town. Guess he should have."

Owen nodded.

"Well, what I'd like to do now—that is, why I'm here is, I'd like to bury him, decently. But it's a tough job, with the ground frozen up. So I was hoping that you might bring over some coal and a few hay bales. There's nothing back at the cabin to make a fire hot enough for thawing the ground."

The man crossed his arms across his chest and let his breath out in a whoosh.

"I would like to help you there, but I can't say that I've got the coal to spare. And I don't know how the horses would do, hauling bales over this heavy snow. Not to mention, my wife won't like it if I up and leave before the turkey's on the table. So, I don't know, really."

Owen looked at the man, who would no longer look him in the eye, and knew that the truth of it was that he didn't want to leave his comfort on Christmas Day. There were a few seconds of awkward silence and then Owen had an idea.

"Do you have a pickax?" he asked.

Owen Piercy worked all of Christmas Day and well into the night, chopping away at the frozen ground. When he had made a hole suitably deep enough for a grave, he carefully wrapped John Spanner's body in a blanket and buried him. Owen said another prayer and filled in the grave, packing the mound down firmly so that the wolves couldn't dig it up.

When he went back into the cabin, it was nearly midnight. Owen was aching and exhausted, and his hands were blistered and raw. Still, there was one more job to do and he meant to do it before he allowed himself to rest.

Owen searched the cabin for a pencil but could not find one. In the end, he made do with a piece of charcoal. He sat at the little makeshift table, turned up the flame on the kerosene lamp and opened the front cover of the leather-bound Bible. There, beneath John Spanner's name and date of birth, Owen scratched out the words *Died December 24, 1933.*

He sat for a moment, looking at the simple inscription. He thought of how John Spanner had surely saved his life and how he had made him so welcome in his home. Owen decided that something more needed to be said, so he hunched over the Bible once more and added the heartfelt three-word epitaph *A Good Man.*

Owen felt a sudden warmth and peace descend upon him, as though someone had placed a large, comforting hand upon his tired shoulder. He closed his eyes, losing himself in the sensation, and it was then that he heard the voice. For one last time, he heard the familiar, hollow voice with its flat British accent, the voice that was somehow inside Owen's head and outside of it at the same time.

*Thank you...*was what it said.

And, then, as Christmas Day drew to a close, it was Owen Piercy's turn to speak. In a voice that was weary and husky with emotion, he returned the kind assurance that John Spanner had repeatedly given him.

"You're very welcome," Owen said softly as he closed the Bible and turned down the flame on the lamp. "You're very welcome, indeed."

The Portrait

Russell Roberts was an artist who lived in a few cramped rooms behind the cluttered studio where he painted for pleasure and profit. His girlfriend often complained that there was too *much* pleasure and too *little* profit in the whole equation. She liked to tell Russell that it was worthless to have an eye for composition if it was not set in a head for business.

"You really make very little money," she said critically each time she pored over the messy scribblers and stacks of receipts that passed for Russell's accounting books.

Russell always shrugged.

"I get by. And I enjoy what I do. That's profit enough," he always replied.

For him, it *was* enough. He liked to paint and he generally liked the people whom he met in his line of work. Because of that, he was often content to let his clients pay him over time or when they could afford to or, sometimes, not at all. But his girlfriend, who wished every Christmas for a more obedient beau and a sparkling diamond ring, saw Russell's way of doing business as foolish.

"If you want to do well, you have to be more shrewd," she told him. "You're entirely too trusting."

Russell supposed that his girlfriend was right but made no real effort to change. He preferred to trust people and found that when he did, he was rarely disappointed by them.

One December day, Russell was invited to attend a Christmas party at the home of his girlfriend's parents.

He was given explicit instructions regarding his attire and behavior for the event.

"Arrive on time, not a minute late," his girlfriend said. "And dress smartly, as though you're on your way to a serious meeting. Try to speak intelligently. And pretend that your business is more successful than it is—I'd *die* if my family found out what a measly living you really make."

Russell nodded in his good-natured way and promised that he'd do his best.

On the night of the function, he squeezed into a pair of dress pants that had grown uncomfortably snug around his waist, put on some stiff leather shoes that pinched his toes and buttoned up the one white shirt that he had not stained with paint. He was searching through the mess of his bedroom for the only tie that he owned when a noise in the studio caught his attention. He investigated and discovered a lovely girl in a cream-colored cocktail dress perusing his works-in-progress.

"Hullo!" he said brightly, not sounding irritated at all at having been interrupted. "You know, I'm closed up right now. I thought I locked the door, but I suppose I forgot. I've been told I have no mind for details."

"But obviously you have an eye for them," the girl said with a smile. She turned back to the painting she had been studying. "These are very good. I like this one especially; the way you've captured the quality of the light is marvelous."

"Well, thank you," Russell said with a blush. "I wish I could show you more, but there's this party and I'm running late..."

The girl seemed not to hear him.

"Could you paint my portrait, do you think?"

Russell smiled.

"Of course. We can make an appointment..."

"No, I mean tonight."

Russell tried once more to explain that he had an obligation.

"I'm sorry," he said, and he truly was. "But my girlfriend wants me at this party on time. I don't think she'd be too pleased if I took on a last-minute job."

The girl arched one delicate eyebrow.

"Not even if you were paid double your usual fee?" she asked.

Russell paused. He knew that money was the only thing that could possibly get him excused from attending the party. But the offer made him curious.

"Why would you want to do that?" he asked the girl.

"Because this must be done tonight," she said. "The portrait is to be a Christmas gift for my mother. It's very important to me and would be worth any amount."

Russell thought about the roomful of strangers that awaited him. He thought about making cautious conversation while balancing a cocktail in one hand and a canapé in the other. Then he thought about the colors that he would mix to achieve the unusual shade of blue that he saw in the girl's eyes and the way that he would finesse the paint with a coarse-bristled brush to simulate the wave and texture of her loose, shiny hair.

"Have a seat," he said. "I just need to make a phone call."

Russell's girlfriend was angry only until she heard about the amount of money he would be paid. Then she thought about the diamond ring that shone so brilliantly against the black velvet background of the jeweler's glass case and she became very understanding.

"If you must miss the party, at least it's for a good reason," she said. "Just make sure you get paid up front."

But Russell was already thinking about how he wanted to light the girl, how he wanted to place her on the canvas and which backdrop would best suit the ivory tone of her dress and her pale skin. Payment was the farthest thing from his mind, and he didn't bother to ask for a dime of it in advance.

The sitting went very well. The girl posed and Russell painted late into the evening. Finally, as the hour neared midnight, he invited his model to have a look at what he had created on the canvas.

"It's wonderful!" she breathed as she gazed at the portrait. "Is it done, then?"

Russell shook his head.

"I need to add a little shading in the background. It needs a few finishing details. But you can go if you like. There's no need to keep you any later than you've already..."

Russell's speech trailed off as he turned to face the girl. She had been standing right beside him, admiring her painting, but suddenly was nowhere to be seen.

"Hullo?" Russell said as he looked around the junky little studio.

"Where did you get to?" he called out as he poked his nose into each of the small rooms of his living quarters.

The girl didn't answer him and she didn't reappear. Eventually, Russell had to assume that she had simply, quickly, quietly left. Her slippery exit baffled him, though. When he went to the front to see if he could spot anyone up or down the street, he noticed that the door was still bolted from the inside. How the girl had gotten in and out was a mystery—but Russell had limited interest in mysteries when there was painting to be done. He returned to the easel and picked up his brush and set about finishing the portrait.

The next morning, Russell's girlfriend was furious.

"So you missed my parents' party and you didn't make a penny," she seethed.

"I'm sure I will," Russell assured her. "She'll be back for the painting after all."

"You don't *know* that!" the girlfriend shrieked. "And, even if she does come back, she'll likely have some hard-luck story about how she can't pay you double any more or can't pay you *at all*. Then you'll say 'Oh, well, the painting's done, so you might as well take it,' and there'll be one more entry in the unpaid accounts!"

Russell let his girlfriend rant but paid no particular attention to what she was saying. He was looking appraisingly at the portrait, which he had hung in the office opposite his small desk.

"It's nice, though, isn't it?" he asked. "Turned out well, I think."

The girlfriend barely bothered to glance at the painting.

"I hate it," she said, "because it reminds me of what a fool you can be. You should take it down and in its place hang a sign that reads 'TRUST NO ONE.' "

Russell winced.

"That's a bit of a harsh approach to life," he said.

"But it ensures that you get paid," she said flatly as she left.

The rest of the morning passed, the lunch hour came and went and the afternoon plodded on as afternoons tend to do. As the end of the business day drew near, Russell began to wonder whether he ever would see the pretty girl in the cream-colored dress again.

Perhaps people can't be trusted, he thought unhappily. But he didn't really think it to be true and wasn't prepared to give up on the girl so soon.

Russell was distracted from his musings by the sound of the front door. He turned to see a well-dressed gentleman walk into his studio. When he walked up to greet the man, Russell noticed that his eyes were the most unusual shade of pale blue.

The man had come with a special request.

"Can you paint a portrait from a photograph?" he asked.

Russell wrinkled his nose a little and shrugged.

"I can do it, but it's difficult," he admitted. "You might not be satisfied with the result."

"I'm willing to take a chance," the man said. "It's for my wife, for a Christmas present. She's always wished to have a portrait of our daughter. If you could do this—and finish it in time for Christmas—I'd be willing to pay twice your usual fee."

The man's offer reminded Russell of the previous evening and the fact that he might have been duped.

"I hate to say this," said Russell, "but it would have to be in advance."

"Of course," said the man, nodding in agreement. "In advance."

He took out a sleek leather billfold and counted out a thick stack of bills. Russell took the money with an embarrassed little nod of gratitude and stuffed it into his pocket.

"May I see the photo?" he asked.

From his briefcase, the man produced a large manila envelope and handed it to Russell. Russell opened the flap, pulled out the photo and had to stop himself from laughing. It was a picture of the girl who had been in to see him the night before.

Russell wasn't sure how to tell the man that he and his daughter had concocted identical plans for his wife's Christmas present. So instead, he posed a sly question.

"Why is it that your daughter won't come in for a portrait sitting?" he asked.

The man's answer was unexpected.

"She's dead," he said, bluntly. "Died in an accident, years ago. So I'm afraid the photo is all you have to work with. Will you be able to deliver the portrait in time for Christmas?"

Russell knew that he could deliver the portrait that very moment but had no idea how he would explain it to the man. So he nodded thoughtfully instead and told the fellow to come back the next day.

By the next day, he reasoned, his hands would no longer be shaking and he could trust himself to take the painting down from his office wall.

Twenty-four hours later, the man returned to Russell's studio.

He was thrilled with his daughter's portrait.

"I don't know how you did it, working from a photograph," he gushed, "but you've truly managed to capture her spirit. Her expression is exactly as I remember it! Her eyes and her hair—it is as though she were here! My wife will adore this!"

Russell spoke his modest thanks, but the man was not done praising him.

"Every detail is perfect," he went on. "That dress—I am tempted to reach out and stroke the fabric! And how she loved that dress. It was her favorite. We buried her in it," he confided to Russell.

The man had driven halfway home with the carefully wrapped canvas propped on the passenger seat beside him before it dawned on him that his daughter had not been wearing her burial dress in the photo he had given Russell Roberts.

"So you *did* sell the painting?"

"Yes, for double my usual fee."

"Well. That's good. I'm happy to hear it."

Russell's girlfriend didn't look happy, however. She was chewing on her lip, frowning in the way that she tended to frown on those rare occasions when she was proven wrong.

"You *are* lucky to have been paid for it at all," she finally said. "I didn't think it was your best work. If I were you, I'd be happy just to have it off my office wall."

"Oh, that reminds me!" Russell said, brightly. "I hung a sign in that spot across from the desk, like you suggested! Kind of a credo, to remind me what's important."

The girlfriend was terribly pleased by this and flounced off to the office to have a look for herself.

My influence is finally taking hold, she thought. *I'll turn him into a success yet, and then I'll have my diamond ring.*

But when she walked into the office and saw the sign, her smug smile faded. She knew that she was not really changing Russell and that she was unlikely to find a velvet jeweler's box beneath the Christmas tree.

There, on a rectangle of canvas, Russell had painted two words with a flourish.

TRUST YOURSELF, they read.

And Russell's girlfriend feared that he always would.

Leo Watkins, Christmas 1952

"Want a chocolate?"

"I don't snack in between meals."

"C'mon, it's Christmas."

"Why is that a reason? Am I the only one who thinks it's insane to toss away every sensible rule that we live by for the sake of the so-called 'festive season'?"

"Yes. You're pretty much alone there, Fitz."

"Unbelievable. And don't call me that."

Randall Fitzpatrick turned back to his desk and tried to concentrate on the spreadsheet that was before him. It wasn't easy to do—not in the midst of a multitude of seasonal distractions. His office mate, Larry, kept rustling through the empty paper wrappers in the massive box of candy he kept on his desk, in search of the remaining, increasingly elusive, soft-centered pieces. Annoyingly joyous carols were being piped over the intercom system. Perky people kept poking their heads through the door to wish Larry and Randall a Merry Christmas. And it was cold. It was *freezing* cold.

"Man, would it be too much to ask for some *heat* in here?" Randall complained as he fiddled with the thermostat for the third time that afternoon. "These are like Dickensian work house conditions!"

"I'm toasty," Larry volunteered cheerfully around a mouthful of chocolate.

"Well, of course, you're toasty," Randall griped. "You're stoking your internal furnace with nuts and fondant every five minutes, plus you're dressed like a Nepalese climbing guide. You are aware that we have a dress code?" He pointed back and forth between his own conservative gray suit and Larry's bulky, handmade snowflake sweater.

"It's Christmas!" Larry laughed.

Randall threw his hands up in the air.

"Again, like that's a reason." He turned the collar of his suit jacket up for extra warmth and stormed out of the room.

Larry caught up with him in the hallway.

"Goin' to the lunchroom, Fitz? I thought I'd go past the lunchroom. Dolores said that Tammy brought in some brownies."

Larry tended to follow Randall around like a puppy. Randall wasn't as bothered by it as he let on; it gave him a sounding board upon which to vent at any given moment of the day.

"You see, it's not just our office. It's cold in the hallway, too," he griped. "You could make ice cubes in this hallway."

Larry chuckled. He was as impossibly good-natured as Randall was acerbic.

"Well, it's a historic building, you know. You're gonna get drafts. Especially in December."

"Yeah," snapped Randall, " 'historic.' You know what 'historic' means? It's a euphemism for 'should have been leveled 20 years ago!' We should be in one of those glass-and-concrete towers, like that over there."

Larry looked out the window across the street at the sleek, modern skyscraper that Randall had pointed at. He scrunched his face in an expression of disapproval.

"Nah," he said. "It's got no character."

"It's got *heat*," Randall hissed as he stomped through the door of the lunchroom.

One of the office secretaries was leaving the room as they entered. On her way past Randall and Larry, she pointed to a large pan of fudgy-looking cake that had been set out in the middle of the table.

"Hey, guys," she said, "have a brownie. They've got caramel in them!"

"Thanks," said Randall, "but I was hoping to ward off killer diabetes for another year or two."

"I'll have his!" said Larry, and he piled two large slices, piggyback style, onto a napkin.

Randall poured himself a cup of decaf and looked at Larry in disgust.

"It won't be long before we'll need a new building just to house your expanding snowflakes," he predicted.

Larry laughed and patted his bulging stomach affectionately. At times Randall wondered if it was at all possible to insult him.

"Better give up on your dream of a new office," Larry said. "I can't imagine 'Leo Watkins Financial Group' being in anything other than 'The Historic Watkins Building.' Can you?"

Randall groaned.

"Yeah, I *can*," he said. "And you know what? If Leo Watkins were here today, I bet he could, too! I doubt that he got as far as he did by being sentimental and soft! Nobody makes it in the business world by forming attachments to buildings, people or anything else."

"You have to respect traditions!" Larry protested.

"Traditions die, things change," Randall said. "Except around here." He sank down into the comfort of the sofa that ran along one wall of the lunchroom and wrapped his hands around his coffee cup for warmth.

Larry plunked himself down two cushions away. The aftershock nearly caused Randall's coffee to splash over the rim of his cup.

"That's not true," he said. "Some things have changed with the times."

"Name one," said Randall.

"Well," said Larry, and he nodded at the large, framed, black-and-white photograph that hung on the wall opposite them, "they don't have the office Christmas party in the office anymore."

That much was true. The photo—with its accompanying plaque that read "Leo Watkins, Christmas 1952"—had always hung as a testament to that tradition that had fallen by the wayside. It was a group photo, taken at the sort of Christmas party where people would drink highballs out of their everyday coffee cups and then get frisky with one another in the supply closet. The women had dark, thickly applied lipstick and carefully styled hair. They wore smartly tailored shirtdresses with cinched waists and peplum jackets over pencil skirts. In contrast, the men appeared disheveled and drunken. Their ties had been loosened and their hair, greasy with styling creme, fell in clumps across their foreheads. One heavyset male partygoer, sporting a grin that showed a gap the size of a country mile between his front teeth, had lost his tie altogether. Randall had always imagined that he had traded it for the corny Santa Claus hat that was perched crookedly upon his sweaty head.

"Okay, you're right," Randall admitted. "One point for you. They *don't* have those ridiculous parties in the office anymore. But they *do* still have them—and everyone gets just as drunk and just as stupid. They just do it in a hotel banquet room, instead of here."

Larry swallowed a large mouthful of brownie and shook his head.

"I can't believe that you hate everything about Christmas as much as you say you do," he said.

"In a way, you're right," Randall said, as he stood up. "I actually hate it even *more* than I say I do. It's a season of bad music, tacky decorations, insincere sentiments and unnecessary expense. And it's a big distraction. Everyone loses sight of what they should be doing."

"Still, you're coming by for a Christmas drink tonight, right?" Larry looked at his friend hopefully as he used his balled-up napkin to wipe the smears of chocolate off his mouth.

The comment stopped Randall in his tracks. He turned and looked at Larry with an incredulous expression.

"How could you possibly, *possibly* think that?" he asked.

Larry hoisted his bulk off the couch so that he could look Randall in the eye.

"I want you to," he said, sincerely. "Mary wants you to. The kids want to see their 'Uncle Fitz.' And, besides, what else are you going to do?"

"I am *not* your children's 'Uncle Fitz' and, anyway, I have plans," Randall said. "I'm working."

Randall began to walk out of the lunchroom, but Larry grabbed his arm and spun him back around.

"Working!" Larry said in a disgusted tone that he usually reserved for people who ordered their pizza without cheese. "You can't be *working!*"

Randall peeled Larry's thick fingers off his arm.

"Yes, I can," he said. "I plan to take advantage of the one good thing about Christmas, which is the fact that all the type-A, mechanical-rabbit-chasing bean counters will be out of the office for once. It's a great chance to catch up on some work without a thousand interruptions."

Larry shook his head.

"And for that, you're willing to miss Christmas?"

"It's just another day. Don't buy into all that 'fellowship' propaganda, Larry. *This*," Randall said, as he tapped the glass-covered photo of the 1952 office party, "is just a fantasy."

Two hours later, the last of the office staff were leaving. As Larry shrugged into his overcoat and wrapped the long scarf that matched his goofy snowflake sweater around his neck, he kept a sad eye focused upon Randall.

"Are you sure you don't want to come by?" he finally asked. "We're going to bake sugar cookies."

Randall didn't look up from his work.

"As delightful as that sounds," he said, "I'm sticking to my original plan. In 15 minutes, this place will be as quiet as a tomb and I shall have my most productive day of the year."

"Well," Larry sighed, "if you change your mind, you know where to find us. Merry Christmas, Fitz."

"Don't call me that."

Larry didn't hear the remark; he had already gone. At last, Randall Fitzpatrick had been left alone to keep Christmas in his own way.

By 7 PM on that Christmas Eve, the Watkins Building had been deserted by everyone except Randall, who was the happiest he had been all day long. It pleased him so much to be left alone that he didn't even mind the fact that he had nudged the thermostat up twice and yet still had to wrap his wool scarf around his neck to keep his teeth from chattering. Every half hour or so, he paused to marvel at all that he was accomplishing.

"Amazing," he muttered to himself. "If this decrepit old pile of bricks was always this empty, I could learn to like it."

As content as Randall was, however, the building's shadowy nighttime alter ego did have him feeling a little on edge. Occasionally, the water cooler would burble, or a pane of glass would rattle in the wind and it would cause him to nervously jump. Everyday sounds took on an eerie quality when they weren't masked by the hum of human activity.

Worse were the sounds that couldn't easily be identified. Some piece of equipment in an office down the hall from Randall was annoying him with its persistent, irregular clacking. It reminded him of the sound his mother's old, manual typewriter but still, it inspired less nostalgia than it did irritation. Three times, Randall went looking for the source of the noise only to give up in frustration when he could not find it.

"Ignore it," he finally told himself as he settled back down at his desk. "Just like you ignore all the daytime distractions."

At that moment, Randall heard a familiar daytime distraction. The discordant elevator bell rang out hollowly through the halls, announcing an arrival on the fifth floor.

Someone has simply forgotten something and has come back to get it, Randall thought. *They'll be gone in a minute. They won't stay.* But when the muted sounds of voices began to drift through the office, he worried that his plan to work unbothered was in jeopardy.

"Who's here?" he seethed. "Who the hell would come back here to work on Christmas Eve?"

Whoever they were, Randall intended to confront them and insist that they work quietly. Before he managed to step out into the hall, however, he was shocked by the appearance of a strange woman who leaned around the door frame.

"Stop working, sugar. It's Christmas Eve," she said.

"What? Who..." stuttered Randall, but he was speaking to an empty room. Just as suddenly as the woman had appeared, she vanished. Randall was left alone and confused. He had never before seen the woman with the bright red lipstick and the dark hair combed in smooth waves.

He walked out into the hall and looked in either direction. He saw nothing but heard a burst of female laughter coming from around a distant corner.

Must be cleaning staff, he finally decided, although it seemed odd to him that they would be working on Christmas Eve. Randall returned to his desk and to his work, but not before turning the thermostat up another degree. His short venture into the hallway had left him shivering with cold.

For a half hour, Randall forced himself to concentrate on his paperwork. It required great effort, however, for the janitors were growing louder and more raucous by the minute. Randall could hear lively conversation and laughter and even snatches of Christmas carols being sung. It finally occurred to him that instead of vacuuming and emptying wastepaper baskets, the cleaning staff were using the offices of Leo Watkins Financial Group as the site of their own private party.

Not for long, Randall thought. He buttoned his suit jacket, straightened his tie and set out to put an end to the revelry.

It was more of a challenge than he imagined it would be.

Every time Randall thought that he was closing in on the unauthorized celebration, it seemed to move. The voices would seem to be just around the corner or just in the next room—but when Randall would arrive on the scene, puffed up and prepared to deliver a nasty speech, he would find that he was utterly alone. After a moment's confusion, he would hear the voices again but from some distant location on the floor.

Randall was beginning to question his hearing and his sanity when, finally, he caught sight of one of the partyers. He was standing at one end of a long corridor when he saw a tall, portly man at the opposite end. The man looked at Randall, nodded slightly, then walked through a doorway and out of sight. He didn't look much like a janitor in his gray flannel suit, but he *did* appear somewhat familiar.

I know you from somewhere, Randall was thinking when he was nearly knocked over by a man and a woman who came running up the hall from behind him.

"Hey!" Randall complained as he grabbed at the wall to keep from falling. "Watch where you're going!"

The couple appeared not to hear him or not to care, for they continued their playful chase. The man grabbed at the woman's waist. As she dodged him, the sound of her laughter rang out loudly. The rhythmic clicking of her heels on the tile floor echoed through the hall.

Somehow, that seemed wrong to Randall. It took him a moment to think of why.

It was because every floor in the Watkins Building had been carpeted over, 30 years before. Randall was *looking* at worn, beige carpeting and *hearing* the distinct click of heels striking tile. The realization made him feel woozy, as though he had quickly downed a very strong cocktail.

"I'm imagining things," he declared out loud and turned back in the direction of his office. Suddenly, though, he found himself imagining many more things, for the hallway was festooned with twisted red and green streamers and ropes of tinsel that hadn't been there before. There were more voices as well, and the sounds of people milling about, though no one was in sight.

Randall's scalp prickled with fear. He stood, back against the wall, conducting a frantic visual search of the hall for the people whose voices were growing closer and louder. Finally, one voice rose above the general din.

"Hey!" it said. "He's under the mistletoe!"

A second later, Randall felt the pressure of invisible, cold lips on his. He let loose a little cry of fear and scrambled backward. Laughter erupted around him.

"Who's there?" he cried. There was no answer, only another burst of laughter that surrounded Randall as if he was in the midst of a gathering that couldn't be seen.

"I'm leaving!" he screamed at whoever it was who was playing the elaborate trick on him. Then, crossing his arms protectively across his face, Randall pushed through the crowd that could be heard but not seen and ran for the safety of his office.

He made it as far as the door before he spotted the mysterious stranger again. Again, the man was standing at the far end of the hall, watching Randall with apparent interest. He was distant enough that Randall couldn't make out the pattern on his tie but was close enough to appear familiar.

"Are you doing this?" Randall yelled down the length of the corridor. "What's going on here?"

The man offered a slight smile, then turned and stepped out of Randall's line of sight.

"*What's going on?*" Randall screamed after him. The man didn't reappear, but someone else answered the question.

"It's a party, pal!"

The voice had come from within the office that Randall and Larry shared. Randall had left the door open only a crack in an effort to hold some heat in the room. With a hand that was trembling and nearly blue with cold, he reached out and pushed the door all the way open.

And he saw that it *was* a party indeed.

There were at least a half-dozen people in the small room. All of them were strangers to Randall and all of them were clearly having a good time. A man and a woman were dancing together in the cramped space between the two desks. Though there was no music that was audible to

Randall, the couple moved fluidly together, with every twitch of their hips perfectly in sync. Another woman sat on Larry's desktop, holding a cigarette and a highball glass, each of which was marked with a vivid print of her red lipstick. Randall saw the smooth waves of her dark hair, heard her call the man she was flirting with "sugar" and recognized her to be the woman who had poked her head in his office earlier.

"Are you comin' in or what?"

It was the same male voice that had spoken to Randall through the nearly closed door; it was the voice that had called him "pal" and informed him that there was a party happening. Randall turned in the direction of the voice and found a young man with crew-cut hair slouching in his specially made ergonomic chair. He had a beer bottle in his hand and his feet were propped comfortably upon the desk, on top of the report that Randall had been working on for more than a week. It was a pose of pure insolence, and suddenly Randall was more angry than afraid.

"Get out!" he yelled. "Out of my office! I'm trying to work!"

The lively chatter stopped. The couple who was dancing twirled to a standstill. But the young man who was occupying Randall's chair only laughed.

"Friend," he said, "haven't you heard? You're not supposed to *work* at a party!"

Randall, who usually chose to do battle with words, took only a second to realize that he needed to physically throw the upstart out of his office. He wanted to see the shock on the kid's face when he was hauled out of the chair, and he wanted to hear the solid sound of his body hitting the wall on the far side of the hallway. It had been a very stressful day, and Randall knew that verbally besting the punk just wouldn't be satisfying enough. He wanted to *hurt* him.

When Randall attempted to grab the trespasser by his jacket lapels, however, *he* was the one slapped with a shock. His hands passed right through the young man's chest and met no resistance until they hit the back of the chair. Randall felt the blood leave his face. The man whose chest he was reaching through began to laugh uproariously and the others in the room joined in. As the laughter grew louder, their images grew fainter, and soon Randall found himself alone in his office, with his frozen hands clamped over his ears in an effort to muffle the deafening roar. His breath was coming in short, panicked bursts, and each exhalation produced a little cloud of icy vapor. When Randall noticed this and waved his hand disbelievingly through the mist, there was a fresh explosion of hysterics from the spectral partyers.

That was when Randall changed his mind and decided to relinquish his office to those who were enjoying it best.

The fifth-floor men's washroom in the Watkins Building featured three sinks, two urinals, two toilet stalls and a door with a deadbolt. The deadbolt had always been a seemingly unimportant fact swimming around in Randall's pool of general knowledge—until that evening, when he burst into the bathroom in a panic and then almost wept with relief as he was able to lock the door behind him. He kicked open the door of each empty stall to confirm that he was alone, then sagged heavily against the cool tile wall and took a moment to collect himself. In the merciful silence of the small, sterile room, he was more easily able to sort out his thoughts. After a while, when his breathing had slowed and his heart had stopped pounding loudly in his ears, Randall reached a conclusion.

"I've lost my mind," he whispered. "I've slipped a gear. This is the big breakdown that I've been waiting for."

He walked over to one of the sinks and turned on the hot tap. He warmed his hands under the gushing faucet first, then bent over to splash handfuls of water on his face. But just as Randall felt his head beginning to clear, the steaming water turned suddenly frigid. He grimaced and pulled his hands out of the icy stream. Then, as he turned off the water, he heard a voice behind him.

"What's the matter, Fitz?"

Slowly, with his face and hands still dripping, Randall straightened up. In the mirror, he saw the rotund man in the gray flannel suit standing behind him, looking over his left shoulder.

"What do you want?" Randall managed to whisper.

The man shrugged casually.

"We're just trying to tell you to loosen up a bit," he said. "Have a little fun. It'll take you farther, in the long run."

The man winked conspiratorially at Randall. There was something so maddeningly *familiar* about his round face and yet Randall couldn't quite place him...

That was until he mentally placed a big Santa Claus hat on top of his shiny, bald head.

Randall's eyes widened in recognition. The man seemed pleased to sense that the puzzle was being pieced together. He smiled into the mirror then, and there it was: the goofy-looking gap, as big as a country mile.

Randall spun around.

"It's *you!*" he said, but he found that he was talking to himself. His voice echoed through the empty room. Randall could see that the deadbolt remained fastened and the stalls were still empty. He turned back to the mirror, but again it showed him nothing out of the ordinary. When he glanced down into the sink, however, he could see a thin frosting of ice on the faucet.

The droplets of water in the basin had frozen solid.

"*Fitz!*"

Larry was still wearing the snowflake sweater but had added a cap with large, fuzzy reindeer antlers to his ensemble. He stood holding the door open with one hand while he balanced a cup brimming with thick, yellow eggnog with his other.

"Come in, come in! I knew you'd come by. Didn't I tell you, Mary? I said, ' I know Fitz; he'll change his mind.' "

"Don't call me that," Randall said as he crossed the threshold, but he said it without much conviction. The fact was that he was happy to be anywhere other than the office and planned to stay, no matter what anyone called him.

Larry's plump, smiling wife appeared and took Randall's coat. Two short, round children in flannel pyjamas smiled at him over the back of the sofa. An overfed dog, lazing in the corner, wagged its tail in a welcoming way.

"I hate to barge in..." Randall said.

Larry interrupted him.

"Who's barging? You were invited! What reeled you in, Fitz? Was it the sugar cookies? Huh? Huh?" Larry picked up a platter of lumpy, pale cookies that had been drowned in red and green icing and waved it under Randall's nose.

Randall tried to look admiringly at the cookies without actually having to touch one.

"Oh, you got me there," he said. "Who can resist pure white refined sugar? But, you know," he added in a low voice, "I kind of wanted to talk to you, too."

"Talk?" boomed Larry. "Sure!"

"No, I mean...*alone*," Randall whispered discreetly.

"Huh? Oh! Right!"

Larry turned to his wife, who had gone back to sticking candy sprinkles on a batch of fresh cookies.

"Honey," he announced importantly, "we'll be in the den."

When the two men were settled in the den—a cramped spare bedroom with an old television and two armchairs that were too threadbare to put in the living room—Randall asked Larry the first serious question that he had ever asked him.

"Do you think I'm rigid?" he said.

Larry frowned and blew out his breath in a sputter.

"No! No, no, no. You? Are you kidding? No!" he laughed. There was a short pause. "Okay, maybe a little," he admitted, "maybe a little 'tense' sometimes. But not 'rigid.' 'Rigid' is a strong word."

"But I could stand to have a little more balance in my life."

"Oh, balance-shmalence. Who really has that figured out?"

"Some people seem to," Randall mused. "Some people work and they have fun, too. I could probably have a bit more fun."

"We're havin' fun right now!" Larry declared, and he toasted Randall with his eggnog.

"Sure," Randall agreed. "Sure, we are. Which will 'take me farther in the long run,' or so I've been told. Of course, he probably spent his whole pathetic life as a junior assistant. Being dead doesn't automatically make him *wise*. What am I listening to a corpse for, anyway?! Can you tell me *that*?"

Apparently, Larry could not, for he was staring at Randall silently, with an expression of mixed confusion and concern. Randall cleared his throat and changed the subject ever so slightly.

"Larry," he said, in a calmer tone of voice, "you know that picture in the lunchroom? The Leo Watkins Christmas party, from the '50s?"

"Yeah, sure," Larry nodded.

"Well—do you have any idea who the fat guy in the back row is? The dufus-looking character with the Santa hat who looks so happy he's about to wet his pants?"

"Yeah, of course."

"Who is he?"

Larry blinked at Randall in disbelief.

"You really don't know?" he said.

"That's why I'm asking." Randall tried to sound patient.

Larry laughed a little.

"That's Leo Watkins," he finally said. " 'Our Founding Father.' Everyone knows that!"

Loosen up a bit. Have a little fun. It'll take you farther in the long run.

Suddenly, the casual words of advice had been given great credence.

"I didn't know that," Randall said in a small, quiet voice. He was thinking about the smiling man in the gray flannel suit. Leo Watkins had gone from balancing his uncle's books to founding "Leo Watkins Financial Group." He had worked out of two sweltering rooms above a Chinese restaurant before building the impressive-for-its-day, five-story Watkins Building. He had made a huge success of his life and he had done so, apparently, without being whipped by the sort of single-minded ambition that Randall had always imagined necessary.

Randall collapsed against the back of the old armchair. He stared at the ceiling, sighed deeply and shook his head.

"I always thought I had to be *serious* if I wanted to get somewhere. I thought it required total *focus*," he said.

There was a moment of silence. When Larry responded, it was in a voice that was several degrees more sincere than his usual jocular tone.

"Not all the time, Randall," he said quietly. "You're smart and you're driven, but you're going to hurt yourself if you don't ease up a little bit."

There was a timid knock at the door, and Larry's small son stepped into the room. He was holding a paper plate with three gooey, tree-shaped Christmas cookies.

"We made these for you, Mr. Fitzpatrick," he said. "They're still warm, out of the oven."

Randall's usual range of cynical responses ran through his head, but none settled on his normally sharp tongue. Instead, he took the plate out of the boy's sticky hands and picked up one of the cookies. He took a bite. It was overwhelmingly sweet, as he had known it would be. But he didn't dislike it as much as he had expected.

Maybe I can eat junk once in a while, he thought. *Maybe I can loosen my tie sometimes. Maybe I'll stop working on holidays.*

"Do you like them, Mr. Fitzpatrick?" the boy asked, politely.

Randall looked up and smiled.

"I like them a lot," he said. Then, as much to Larry as to his son, Randall added, "and you can call me 'Uncle Fitz.' "

Last Stop Mission

Karl's first thought upon opening his eyes was that a heart attack wasn't nearly as bad as people always said. The pain in his chest had been terrible, that was true, and the agonizing lightning bolt that had shot down his arm had convinced him that he was dying. But when he blacked out, there had been sweet nothingness. And when he awoke, he felt better than he had in a long, long time. He wanted to tell the stranger who was helping him to his feet that he really didn't need any help at all.

"That's okay, friend. Don't try talkin' yet. Let's get the snow off you," the man said.

Karl realized then that he had been mumbling, the way he sometimes did when he was drunk, although he hadn't had time to get a buzz going that afternoon. It made him think that the fall had taken a bit of a toll after all. He was a little confused, a little woozy and he decided to let the stranger take care of him until he got his bearings.

The man used his rough, bare hands to brush off Karl's shabby coat. He tugged Karl's partially unraveled wool hat back down over his balding head and handed him his old gloves. Then he led him away from the line of garbage cans in the alley where he'd fallen and out onto the quiet street.

"Easy does it," the man said as they shuffled through the dusting of fresh snow together. "No need to get in a hurry."

The two men had walked nearly half a block before Karl realized that he had lost something.

"My bottle!" he gasped. "I had a bag with a mickey of gin!"

"Now that's quite a coincidence," the stranger mused. " 'Mickey' happens to be my name."

"I gotta go back! I can't lose that—I don't have money for any more!" Karl was frantically patting at the pockets of his coat and trousers as he spoke, but he knew that the paper bag had to be sitting in the snow by the trash. He had been holding it in his hands, about to unscrew the cap and take his first swig, when his chest had exploded with pain.

Mickey, the stranger, tried to calm him.

"We can go back later," he said. "Give yourself a little time."

"Someone else will get it!" Karl insisted, and he turned to go back on his own. But, oddly, although the two men hadn't walked very far, Karl didn't recognize the deserted street he was on. He couldn't see the entrance to the alley anymore, and nothing—not the streetlights, not the buildings, not even the faded signposts—looked familiar. He began to wonder how hard his head had hit the concrete.

"You'll be alright," Mickey assured him. "But we can't go back right now. We have to walk a bit. Are you okay to walk?"

Karl nodded numbly. He had never in his life abandoned a full bottle of liquor, but he was lost and confused and had no choice but to rely upon his new companion.

"You haven't told me your name, friend," Mickey said, once they had started walking, again.

"It's Karl." He didn't bother to give his last name. No one on the street ever did.

"Pleasure to meet you, Karl," said Mickey. "It's lucky that I happened along when I did."

Karl made some vague noise of agreement but wasn't really thinking about how lucky he was. In fact, he was still thinking about the bottle and the distance that was growing between him and it.

"You know, I was goin' somewhere," Karl remembered after the two men had walked in silence for several blocks. "I was goin' over to that shelter on Fifth Street. They have a turkey dinner today—a real good one. There's a lady, always gives me extra gravy."

Mickey shook his head curtly.

"Can't go there," he said.

"Why not?" Karl asked. "It's still Christmas Day, ain't it?" For a frightening moment, he wondered exactly how long he had spent in that blissful unconscious state.

"Sure, it is. 'Course it's Christmas," said Mickey, easing Karl's mind. "But I know a better place. It's closer—just up around the corner here."

Because he was hungry and hopelessly lost, Karl allowed himself to be led along. He followed Mickey around the corner and up the front steps of a narrow brownstone with boarded-up windows.

"Looks deserted," said Karl. There was no light over the door and there were no tracks marring the fresh snow blanketing the stoop. If there was anyone inside, they were being silent as thieves and hadn't bothered to turn on a single light.

"Come on," said Mickey. "It looks different on the inside."

He was right.

The inside of the brownstone was invitingly warm and bright and was humming with human activity. The air was filled with the tempting aroma of roasting meat. Karl could see that, aside from a galley kitchen with a cafeteria-style pass-through window at the back, the main floor had been left as one large, open area. Long, folding banquet tables were set up in rows and metal chairs were scattered around them. Most of the chairs were occupied by the type of people Karl saw every day.

There were some whose hands trembled when they lifted a fork, and some whose speech had been permanently slurred by intoxicants. There were young girls wearing heavy makeup and short skirts in an effort to look older, and women relying on the same props as they tried to appear young. There was one woman, in a patched lumberjack shirt, whose face was marred by pockmarks and several missing teeth. The man who sat beside her, patting her hand and sharing some long, involved story, had thin hair that had been greased back into a ponytail. Blue-gray tattoos snaked out from beneath the frayed cuffs of his shirt. His skinny face was partially obscured by a wispy beard and mustache. There was an old lady in a bizarre, crocheted hat—and Karl knew that she was probably never seen without it. A haggard-looking man wearing denim clothes so faded that they looked bleached was sitting alone, eating his dinner with his right hand while he cradled a small knapsack like a baby in the crook of his left arm. Like the lady with the hat, Karl knew him a little, by type. He knew that the guy not only ate with the knapsack, he also slept with it and went to the john clutching it, too. He probably bathed with it, when he had to—but it looked as though no one had asked him to do that in a while.

"Hey, everybody," Mickey said, as the door closed behind him. "This is Karl. He's new."

The buzz of conversation died down and everyone in the room turned to look at the new arrival. Karl felt uncomfortably warm. He ducked his head a little and raised one hand, timidly.

"Hey," he said. He was unaccustomed to being introduced.

"Hello, Karl," said the woman with the pockmarks. She smiled, showing the gaps in her dental work but also a lovely shine in her brown eyes.

"Make yourself at home, man," said a teen with long, greasy hair and multiple piercings. He held his fist aloft in a gesture of welcome.

"Grab a chair."

"Get a plate."

"Glad to meet you."

Greetings came at Karl from all over the room. The group had looked familiar; they had appeared predictable; but, when they spoke to Karl, he could see that they were really nothing like the folk that he was used to meeting. They seemed happy and content. They had a hopeful air about them.

Karl nodded and smiled shyly. A little at a time, people turned their attention back to their own meals and conversations.

"There's food in the kitchen, if you want some," Mickey said. Karl didn't have to be asked twice. He followed his new friend to the back of the big room and let a round woman in a hairnet and a white apron fill a tin plate for him. Karl watched her mound up the stuffing and mashed potatoes and drown everything in gravy. He was embarrassed when a rivulet of saliva escaped his mouth and he had to wipe his chin on his sleeve.

"Sorry," he said to the woman, as she handed him his tray. "Haven't eaten for a bit."

The woman smiled at him.

"I hear you, honey," she said. "I spent a lotta years on the street myself."

There were two empty chairs at the end of one table. Karl sat in one and Mickey took the other.

"Lucky," noted Karl. "Looks like we got the last two places. An hour from now, we prob'ly woulda be sent somewhere else."

"No, there's always just enough room here," said Mickey. "Fifty chairs, fifty meals and fifty people. Well, fifty-one, tonight, but I'll be moving on, now that you're here."

"I don't wanna take your place or nothin'," said Karl, around a mouthful of food. "You shouldn't have to go on my account. I can't stay anyway." The food was good and the room was welcoming, but he was still thinking about the bottle he had left behind. He would have to get back to it or score another one, before the shakes set in. It was actually surprising that they hadn't already. Karl was mentally craving a drink, but physically he was still okay.

Mickey wouldn't hear of him leaving, though.

"You belong here now," he said. "This is your home until you bring someone in. Then, it'll be your turn to move on. But don't be in too much of a hurry. Like I said before, give yourself some time."

Nothing he said made much sense to Karl, but he'd learned early on that it wasn't as important to understand things as it was to *appear* to understand things. He nodded, said nothing and continued to eat.

After a while, Mickey excused himself and began to move slowly around the room, talking to people. There was much hand shaking and backslapping and hugging. From what Karl could see and the few snatches of conversation that he could hear, Mickey really was planning to leave. He was saying his goodbyes. He moved from one person to the next and the next, until Karl saw him embrace someone that he knew and he almost choked on his buttered roll.

He was a young guy, a wiry junkie with dark, curly hair and faded blue eyes whose name was Pete. Karl had always thought of Pete as a good kid with a bad habit. He'd been more than a little sad when, during a November cold snap, he'd heard that Pete had frozen to death in a Dumpster. He'd assumed that the rumors were true; he hadn't seen the guy in the six weeks since. At least, not until the moment he saw him grasp Mickey's hand to say farewell.

"Pete!" Karl yelled across the room. "Pete!"

Pete looked through the crowd. Karl waved both arms to get his attention. When Pete finally saw him, he smiled in recognition. He said a few more words to Mickey, patted him on the shoulder and then made his way across the room.

"How ya doin', man?" he said as he sat down in the empty chair opposite Karl. "It's good to see you."

Karl shook his head in disbelief as he stared at his young friend.

"Not nearly as good as it is to see you!" he said. "I thought you were a goner! I heard you froze to death!"

Pete smiled.

"Yeah, who would have figured we'd see each other so soon, man? It's weird. But things are good here. You'll like it."

Karl looked around.

"It seems nice," he said. "Nice people. But I gotta get going, soon. Gotta score myself a drink before things get bad. You know how it is."

But Pete was shaking his head, as though he *didn't* know how it was.

"No, Karl, man," he said. "You don't need that any-more."

"What are you talking about?"

"I'm sayin' you don't need it," Pete insisted. "Look at me."

He pulled up the sleeves of his bulky sweater and held his forearms out for Karl to inspect. The track marks were still there, but they weren't of the angry, red, fresh variety. They were fading. The kid was either shooting up in some less visible veins, or he was getting clean. Karl looked into his eyes, saw a light that he had never before seen there, and decided that it was the latter.

"I haven't used since I got here," Pete said. "Just don't need to anymore. And neither do you."

Before Karl could respond, Mickey was back at the table.

"I'm on my way, Karl," he said. "Just need to talk to you for a minute first."

Pete quickly excused himself. Karl expected Mickey to sit in the vacated chair, but instead, he motioned for Karl to follow him over to an unoccupied corner of the room.

"It's important," he explained, when Karl looked at him questioningly. "Let's get away from the noise."

Karl followed Mickey into the corner, away from the crowd. When they got there, Mickey took a frayed, dirty-looking business card out of his pocket and pressed it into the palm of Karl's hand. There were three words on the front of the card, in black, block letters. They read **LAST STOP MISSION.**

Karl shook his head.

"What's this for?"

"Today, I brought you in," Mickey explained. "So this is yours, now, until you bring somebody else in."

"It's like a membership card, or somethin'?"

That made Mickey laugh.

"Sure, sort of," he said. "You'll figure it out soon enough. It's better if you get it a little at a time."

Karl looked at the card. It had been white at one time, he could tell, but a thousand dirty fingerprints had turned it dull gray. He wondered how many hands had held the card and how many times it had been passed forward. He thought of stuffing it into his pocket and forgetting about it, but that seemed dishonest. Mickey had been good to him; he could at least be straight in return.

"I can't keep it," he said, and he handed the card back to Mickey. "You should give this to someone who can stay."

The look on Mickey's face told Karl that no one had ever before refused membership to the mission.

"Karl," said Mickey, "you're *here*. You can't...I mean, you'd just end up wandering..."

Karl shrugged and smiled.

"That's what I do," he said, and he turned to walk away. He managed to take only one step before Mickey grabbed his arm and spun him around. Suddenly, Karl found himself pinned against the wall, with Mickey's intense eyes only inches away from his own.

"Listen," Mickey said, "we're not like other folks. There's no one to take care of us, so we have to take care of each other, understand?"

Karl shook his head. Mickey groaned in frustration. Then he looked at Karl for a long time and finally seemed to come to a decision.

"I guess I gotta come right out and explain something to you," he said, levelly, "so pay good attention, friend. A lot of the time, there are no funerals for us. No last rites, no prayers, no markers on the graves. All that ceremony—it's more important than you'd think. A person can get lost without it. So we take care of each other, okay?"

Mickey backed off then and released his grip on Karl. He tucked the worn card into the breast pocket of Karl's shirt.

"I still don't get it," whispered Karl.

Mickey patted his shoulder roughly.

"You will," he promised. "Just stay here; give yourself some time. Before you know it, you'll bring someone in and it'll be your turn to move on."

And then Mickey left. He walked away from Karl and disappeared through a rear door near the kitchen. For a minute, Karl simply stared after him. He watched the door swing slowly shut behind him. And then, suddenly, he decided that he wasn't finished asking questions.

"What are you talkin' about?" he muttered, under his breath. Then, more loudly, "*What the hell are you talkin' about?*"

But the door had closed, Mickey was gone and the only way Karl was going to get any answers was if he went after him. So he did.

Karl walked to the back of the room and through the door. It took his eyes a minute to adjust to the dim lighting on the other side. When they did, Karl saw that he wasn't in a room, really; the door had opened to a narrow, poorly illuminated stairwell. Mickey wasn't there on the tiled landing, so he had to have gone up the stairs. Karl grabbed the creaky, wooden banister and started to climb.

The stairs went on forever.

Karl knew that it probably just seemed that way; he wasn't in the best of shape, after all. Still, there was flight after flight winding up through the building that he could have sworn looked like an ordinary two-story structure from the outside.

Karl climbed until his thigh muscles burned and his feet felt like lead. He climbed until his breathing was labored and his heart thumped loudly in his chest. He was marveling at the fact that he could do it at all when his ticker had given out on him just a few hours earlier, and he was wondering whether it would be wise to sit down for a rest when he finally saw the top of the staircase. At the top of the staircase, he saw Mickey.

Mickey, however, did not appear to see him. He was standing on a small landing in front of a single, nondescript door, the only thing to which the staircase led. His head was bowed slightly and his eyes were closed. He was standing so quietly and looking so reverential that Karl didn't immediately call out to him. Instead, he sank down on one of the steps where he could quietly watch. It felt a little shameful and voyeuristic, but Karl was too curious to turn away.

Mickey stood there, in prayerful silence, for a minute or two more. Then he raised his head, opened his eyes and took a deep breath. The door swung open before him.

Then Karl saw something the likes of which he had never seen in his entire life.

Radiant, white light burst through the doorway. It washed over Mickey and flooded the stairwell. Karl could feel that it was somehow more than just ordinary light; it was warm, welcoming and inviting. Still, it nearly overwhelmed Karl with its intensity. He held his arm up to shield his face against the brilliance. Through squinting eyes, he was able to see that Mickey was being less cautious. Mickey was drinking it in; he was absorbing it; he had his head tilted back and his arms spread wide. The lines in his face had melted away and tears were beginning to trickle down his cheeks.

"Mickey!" Karl called to him.

Mickey looked back once, briefly, and smiled. Karl could see that his features appeared to be lit from within. He only saw for a moment, however, before Mickey turned back to the beautiful, blinding light. He stepped across the threshold and vanished inside the magnificent brilliance.

Then, to Karl's horror, the door began to swing shut.

"Mickey, wait!" Karl screamed. "I'm comin', too! Hang on!"

Suddenly, he was desperate to be in that lovely, glowing place. He wanted to have that warmth spill over him and feel the pain and the years seep out of his body. Karl scrambled to his feet and clambered up the last flight of stairs. He tripped once, landing painfully hard on his elbows. He scarcely noticed, he was so intent upon getting to the light.

"Mickey!" he called frantically. "Wait up!"

Karl made it to the top landing. He reached forward and felt a sliver of light caress the rough, callused skin of his hand. But it was only for an instant. The door was slowly closing; the stairwell was growing more and more dark. The bar of light that Karl could see between the door and its frame was narrowing by the second.

"Please!" he sobbed, as he grabbed at the edge of the door.

For a moment, he thought he had it. But the door was heavy, heavier than it looked, and it slipped through his fingers and slid tightly into place. Karl heard a soft "click" as it latched.

"*No!*" he wailed, as he pounded on it, loudly. "*Let me in!*"

There was one magnificently hopeful moment when he thought that perhaps the door was only closed and not locked. But when he searched feverishly for a doorknob, his hands felt nothing but smooth, dry wood. Karl took a step backward and could see that there was no knob, no handle, no way of opening the door from his side.

"Karl..."

From somewhere very far away, his name was being called.

"Karl!" It sounded closer, much closer, the second time. Karl reluctantly turned around. He saw that Pete had followed him up the stairs and knew, instantly, that he was going to try to talk him into going back.

"Where's the key?" Karl begged him. "There's gotta be a special key or somethin'. There's no doorknob."

"Come back downstairs and we can talk about it," Pete said.

"The *key!*" Karl cried in a voice more pleading than demanding.

Pete looked at him sympathetically.

"You'll get it, Karl. We all will, in turn. When you bring someone in, man, that's your key. *That's* your key. But all in good time."

And that was when things began to slip into place in Karl's head. That was when he truly understood that if he went back to look for his bottle of gin, there would be more than just an impression in the snow where he had fallen. His body would be there, his face would be twisted in a mask of heart-stopping pain, and his blank eyes would be staring heavenward.

All in good time.

Karl reached into his breast pocket and felt the fuzzy, paper edge of the card that Mickey had given him. He wondered how long it would be before he was able to pass it on to someone else.

Pete spoke to him as though he had read his thoughts.

"It'll happen soon enough, man," he said. "And this is a good home for us, now. It's a place where we can help each other get used to the idea, you know? A place where we can take some time to let go."

Karl didn't speak for a long time. He understood what Pete was telling him, but it didn't make it any easier to walk away from the door.

"Been a long day," he finally blurted out, with a humorless little laugh.

Pete smiled with relief.

"I know," he said. "Come on, now. We're gonna sing some Christmas carols."

Karl nodded and he joined Pete on the stairs. The walk down seemed even longer and more arduous than the walk up had been, but it was alright. Karl knew that, when the time was right, he'd be going back up.

In the warm room that was known to a select number of souls as the "Last Stop Mission," carols and hymns were sung well into the dark night. Many of the voices were raspy from years of booze and cigarettes. Many others were shrill or simply tuneless. The guy with the knapsack couldn't remember all of the right words, so he made some up as he went along. The old lady with the crazy-looking hat didn't sing at all, but thumped out an irregular rhythm on the table. The overall effect was sort of dragging and discordant.

But to Karl, they sounded like angels.

Not All Bad

Desmond Marcus didn't like kids and he didn't like Christmas, but the Santa Claus gig at the mall paid 40 dollars a day, which he could ill-afford to turn down while he was otherwise unemployed. He told the fat, mouth-breathing, cheap suit–wearing assistant mall manager that he would take the job, reasoning that it would be easier, overall, than asking his judgmental, uncharitable brother for another loan to see him through the holiday season.

"Anyone can do anything for three weeks," Desmond told himself on the first day, as he donned layers of hot, itchy, red polyester and strapped a pillow to his skinny frame.

But, by that afternoon, he was willing to admit that he might have been wrong.

He was jumped on, prodded at, pinched and punched by horrible yuppie offspring of all ages and sizes. The really big ones always wanted to bounce on his lap until his thighbones were threatening to fracture, and the small ones clawed at him with their little razor fingernails while they wailed for their overindulgent mothers. They all demanded, in their whiny, nasally, high-pitched voices, that he bring them toys and chocolates and other things that they surely didn't deserve. Those who didn't immediately spew out their wish lists were usually older brats, who first wanted to challenge Desmond's authenticity.

One boy, who had been dressed in a jaunty little suit to have his photo taken with Santa Claus, yanked Desmond's flowing, synthetic beard away from his face and then let it go with a stinging elastic snap.

"You're not the *real* Santa Claus," he complained in a petulant tone.

"No," Desmond said. "You're right." Then, just before the picture was snapped, he added in a low, conspiratorial voice, "The real Santa Claus is dead."

The expression that the horrible child was wearing in the photo gave Desmond his one shining moment of Christmas cheer in an otherwise dismal day.

Generally, though, the photographs were the worst.

Some kids pressed their sticky little chocolate-coated mugs against his jacket and refused to look at the camera. Others howled the instant the camera was pointed at them. And, no matter how badly behaved or photographically traumatized the child, Desmond was expected to make things work.

"Come on, already, bounce your knee a bit!" snapped the girl in the elf suit who took the pictures. "Give it a little 'ho-ho-ho!' That's what you're paid for!"

"And paid handsomely, too," Desmond replied through teeth clenched in another happy-Santa-photo smile. He amused himself for the remainder of the day by planning the elf's slow and agonizing death.

Sadly, there were very few slow moments during which he could devote himself entirely to formulating the evil plan. More often than not, a line of urchins extended all the way around the mall's "Christmas Wonderland" and past the one-hour photo-mart.

And then there was the one, lone kid who spent much of the afternoon just hanging around the perimeter.

Desmond had noticed him before his lunch break—a boy of about 10 or 11, standing away from the crowd with his hands stuffed casually into the pockets of his quilted vest. He watched the other kids with great interest but made no move to join them.

Not as much of a sheep as the others, Desmond had thought admiringly at one point. Still, it wasn't enough to inspire him to be friendly when the boy approached him at the end of the day.

"You don't look like you're having much fun," the kid said, as Desmond closed off the cattle chute with a moth-eaten velvet rope.

"Really!" Desmond snorted. "Astute of you to notice. Now, get lost. We're closed."

The kid wasn't that easily put off, though. He tagged along behind Desmond as he pulled the gym bag that held his street clothes from beneath the elf's curtained table.

"Don'tcha like Christmas?" he asked.

"Not a bit," Desmond admitted.

"Come on," urged the kid. "There must be *something* about it that you like."

Desmond paused. The kid was persistent, but in a genuine way that made him less irritating than the scores of spoiled progenies that he had dealt with through the day. He decided to give him an answer.

"There is one thing I like about Christmas," he said. "*Only* one thing. I like eggnog, if it's been thinned out with plenty of amber rum, so I can get cross-eyed enough that I don't have to witness all of the ridiculous seasonal goings-on."

The kid laughed. Desmond started off down the mall, toward the employee washrooms, where he could change back into something that didn't give him a rash. The kid didn't follow but called after him.

"There, you see?" he said, cheerfully. "It's not all bad!"

" 'Not all bad' my butt," muttered Desmond, who had never, in his life, responded well to optimism.

As the days dragged by, Desmond frequently noticed the kid hanging around the sidelines, lurking in the periphery of his vision. It was more than a week, however, before the two spoke again.

Desmond was wiping some two-year-old's vomit off the front of his suit with a paper towel dipped in club soda when the boy walked up to the ratty, velvet rope that separated Santa Claus from the general mall population. He stood silently for a minute or two, waiting for Desmond to acknowledge his presence.

"Here again?" Desmond finally asked. He put a little less than the usual amount of sneer in his voice.

"Yeah," said the kid. "I like the mall at Christmastime. I like looking at the decorations, mostly."

Desmond shook his head. Why anyone would choose to be in the mall when they didn't have to be was beyond him.

"Decorations!" he said. "That's pathetic. Don't your mom and dad put up a tree?"

"Not anymore," said the kid.

Desmond rarely felt sympathetic toward anyone—he generally found people to be miserable complainers who made their own bad luck—but the kid's simple comment sounded sad to him. Cynical as he was, he couldn't imagine people who were too self-involved to put up a Christmas tree for their child.

"Well, listen," he said, gruffly, "I'm on a break, but if you want to grab a candy cane out of the bucket, it's alright by me."

"Hey, thanks," the kid said. Then, as an encouraging, parting shot, he added "Remember, it's not all bad."

And then the kid was gone. Desmond looked to see *where* he had gone so quickly, but some mall-rat skater-kid was suddenly in his face, blocking his field of vision, asking which way it was to the food court. By the time Desmond had blown him off, the kid was nowhere to be seen.

He stayed on Desmond's mind, though. *Decent kid*, he thought, when he was on his way home that night. Those were two words he had never put together before.

Desmond saw the kid a few times after that, but always from a distance and always at a time when he was pinned down by a lapful of runny-nosed brats. He didn't get to actually speak to him again until the mall was about to close on Christmas Eve.

"Okay, you have to admit—it wasn't all bad, right?"

Desmond, who had thought he was the last living person in "Christmas Wonderland," jumped and hit his head on the gift-laden, painted, plywood sleigh. Ordinarily, he would have verbally taken a piece out of the person who had startled him—but he was happy to be finished with the worst job he had ever had and he was happy to see the kid, so he let it go.

"All bad? No," he said, with a bit of a grin. "It was just 99.9 per cent bad. What are you doing here, anyway? Everything's closed up."

The kid shrugged. Desmond wondered where it was that he went when he wasn't hanging out at the mall.

"I'm all out of candy canes," he said, apologetically. He was wishing that there was something else he could give the kid when an idea came to him.

"Hey!" he said. "You want a photo?"

"I got no money," the boy said, although the look on his face told Desmond that if he had had three bucks, he would have gladly spent it on having his photo taken with Santa.

"That's okay," Desmond assured him. "This one's on the house. Come on."

Desmond sat down, for one last time, in the oversized wing chair that had been his official throne for three hellish weeks. He patted his knee and the kid sat down—or, perhaps, he simply leaned against Desmond's knee, for he felt light as a feather. Desmond picked up the remote camera device that he used whenever the nasty elf was on a smoke break and draped his other arm around the boy's slight shoulders.

"Okay," he said. "Say 'Merry Christmas!' "

The kid smiled, Desmond pushed the button, the camera flashed, and it spit out its Polaroid picture.

"Thanks!" the kid said. It was obvious that he was genuinely delighted. "That was pretty cool of you!"

"Well, wait a minute, now," Desmond said. "Don't go running off and forget your picture." He took the milky, still-developing photo off the camera stand and turned around to hand it to the kid.

But the kid was gone. The kid was gone, and Christmas Wonderland was deserted. So was the rest of the mall, for as far as Desmond Marcus' eyes could see.

It took the Polaroid a minute to develop. By the time it did, Desmond wasn't completely surprised by what it showed. It was a photo of himself, alone, with his arm encircling a hazy ball of diffused light.

It took half an hour before Desmond felt calm enough to change out of the polyester torture device. That made him a half hour late turning his gear in to the assistant mall manager, who was already cranky about having to work on Christmas Eve.

"We had four complaints about you," the man huffed, "and we only did about 75 per cent of the photo business that we did last year. The elf says you're difficult to work with and you got a big stain on the front of the suit here."

Desmond raised one sarcastic eyebrow.

"Are you done?" he asked. "Can you give me my money and let me out of this retail hole?"

"No!" the man said, as he jabbed a pudgy finger in Desmond's direction. "I'm not through. I wanted to tell you that you did a barely passable job, *barely* passable, do you hear? But...It's hard to find anyone willing to do this. So, can we call you next year?"

Desmond thought of the biting, the pinching, the punching and the puking; he thought about the red-faced, wailing toddlers with undependable bladders and the insolent pre-teens armed with joy-buzzers and water pistols. He thought about the bitchy elf, the self-righteous parents and the irritating middle-management goof who was wheezing across the desk from him at that very moment, putting every ounce of his minor authority on grand display.

And then he thought about the Polaroid picture that he had tucked safely into his breast pocket.

"Sure," he said to the assistant manager, "you can call me." He collected his wages then and turned to leave. But there was something else that needed to be said.

"You know what?" he said to the puffed-up little man behind the desk. "This was the worst job I've ever had."

The assistant manager shot him a look of contempt.

"So why did you say you'd do it again?" he sneered.

Desmond gave a little shrug and walked out the door. A few moments later, speaking to no one in particular, he finally answered the question.

"'Cause it was not all bad," he said, as he patted the pocket of his shirt. "Not all bad at all."

Part Two:
Family

"It is in the love of one's family only that heartfelt happiness is known."

—Thomas Jefferson

The Christmas Card

"Millie! I near forgot! You got some mail."

Millie Benn had been halfway out the front door and into the brilliant December sunshine. She turned around, squinting as she had when she had first walked into the gloomy little general store.

The large woman who spent her days perched on a high stool behind the counter stood up stiffly and waddled six steps to the place where she kept neat little stacks of mail in a bank of cubbyholes. Before she had even pulled the envelope completely out of the box that always held Millie's mail, Millie recognized the slant of the handwriting.

"Oh, that looks like my Christmas card from Laura!" she said. She held out her hand to receive it. "Thanks, Darlene."

Darlene smiled and hoisted her bulk back onto the stool.

"You hear from your sister often?" she asked. She was making small talk. She knew that Laura sent Millie a birthday card and a Christmas card every year. Nothing more. She also knew that—unless she was mailing things in town—Millie sent exactly the same in return.

"No, not terribly often. Now and then, you know." Millie answered with the practiced vagueness she used whenever anyone asked about Laura. She didn't care to go into detail with acquaintances about how Laura had married a man who kept her tightly under his thumb and discouraged contact with her old friends and even her family. She didn't wish to explain that the sister who had once shared every detail of her life had withdrawn a little more each year until, eventually, she only sent greeting cards to mark special occasions. Millie remained vague because she preferred to keep her private life private and because she believed that people often asked questions when they weren't particularly interested in the answers anyway.

This seemed to be the case with Darlene.

"Well, that's nice she keeps in touch," she said. She had begun to thumb through the TV listings that she always kept on the shelf under the counter. Her television was carefully placed so that she could sit behind the counter and see it through the wide doorway that connected the store to the sitting room of her living quarters. Darlene was able to watch the soaps and game shows all day long as she handed out mail and sold the odd tin of beans or package of stale cookies off the dusty shelves.

Millie nodded and tucked the card into the side pocket of her purse.

"Well, I'd better get a move on," she declared. "It's nearly lunch time; I can't believe how the time goes!"

Darlene nodded and drawled her standard "Bye-bye now," but the weather-beaten door with the bell on the back had already slammed shut behind Millie. By the time Darlene looked up, Millie was climbing behind the wheel of her tough old pickup truck. Within seconds, the vehicle had roared to life and was cutting a fresh set of tracks through the snowy incline that led up to the road.

Darlene shook her head. *People sure do get themselves in a hurry*, she thought. She preferred her own life, which rarely required her to go anywhere, let alone go anywhere in a hurry.

The truth was, Millie wasn't really concerned about lunch or the time of day. She was retired, she lived alone and she spent her time as she pleased. She ate when she was hungry, slept when she was tired, and when she wanted to hurry home to sit at her sunny kitchen table with a cup of black tea and a card from her nearly estranged sister, that was what she did.

Within 20 minutes, she was there. The truck had been parked, the sugar and canned milk purchased from Darlene had been put away and Millie was at the table with her favorite mug and the oversized envelope before her. It was her habit to prolong the anticipation of reading a card or letter, so she didn't open it for several minutes. Instead, she sipped her tea and stared out through the wide kitchen window at the five pretty acres that were all that remained of the land she and her husband had once farmed. Then, when she could wait no longer, Millie began slowly by reading the envelope. She always felt that a person could tell a lot by reading an envelope if that person took the time to read more than just the words.

Laura's envelope was made of heavy paper. It was stiff, textured and likely expensive. The color was an icy shade of pale blue, which told Millie that the foil lining of the envelope would be silver. Over the years, she had learned that Laura favored cool-colored envelopes with silver foil or warm colors with gold. She never chose anything that had red or green foil, not even at Christmastime. Millie imagined that her sister thought of the vivid colors as gaudy. Laura had always been concerned about appearances. Hence the tasteful envelope, the immaculate handwriting, the little snowflake sticker perfectly centered over the flap of the envelope, sealing it in place. The stamp, however, was crooked. It had the appearance of having been stuck on hastily by a thumb that was dirty enough to leave a dull smudge on the otherwise pristine card. Millie laughed a little and clucked her tongue.

"Laura, Laura, Laura," she chastised aloud. "Little details make all the difference!" It was a gentle criticism that Laura had often given Millie in the days when they were close.

"Millie, you can't wear brown shoes with a gray wool skirt," she would say or "Millie, don't go into town without bothering to put on a touch of lipstick."

"Why does it matter?" Millie would always ask as she shrugged her shoulders. "What difference does it make?"

Laura's response was always the same.

"Little details make all the difference," she would say in a tone that indicated there was nothing else to say.

And now, here she was throwing stamps on askew and with dirty hands to boot. Millie had to laugh. And she chose to take it as a good sign, a sign that Laura was loosening up a little, learning to throw caution to the wind. Who knew? Maybe someday she would be able to pick up the phone and call Millie without first asking permission from her sour, overbearing husband.

Millie put the thought of Laura's husband out of her mind as she used her fingernail to tear open the back of the envelope. She didn't want anything to spoil her fun.

The foil lining was silver, as Millie had known that it would be. The card itself was a pale watercolor picture in shades of blue and gray, depicting the Baby Jesus in his bassinet of straw. Through the manger door shone the

Christmas star, in raised silver foil that matched that on the envelope. It was a pretty picture, but Millie barely looked at it. She was too eager to get to what was inside.

What was inside proved to be a disappointment.

Millie's mood sank a little the very moment she opened the card, when no folded sheets of stationery fell out. Usually, there was a newsy letter enclosed. Millie was even more disheartened to see that the blank side of the card contained only a spare paragraph in Laura's perfect handwriting.

> Dear Millie—
> Where does the time go? I'm worried that if I don't get these cards done now, they never will be done, so forgive the absence of my usual, rambling letter. It's been a year of changes and I promise to fill you in on the details eventually.
> Have a merry Christmas!
> All my love,
> Laura

It's a good thing I took the time to read the envelope, Millie thought bitterly. *There was more to it.* She was so upset by the card that she stuffed it back in its envelope and tossed it on the kitchen counter by the telephone, where the bills and junk mail and stray bits of paper tended to collect. She knew that she would display it on the mantle eventually, with the other Christmas cards. But for the time being, Millie did not want to be reminded of how annoyed and hurt she was by the impersonal, hasty note.

Three days later, Millie had nearly forgotten about the card. She was reminded when she stopped in to collect her mail and saw the familiar, gray-blue paper among the stack of envelopes that Darlene handed her. It had to be the nice long letter that Laura had promised. As she drove home over the rutted, icy back roads, Millie felt uncomfortably guilty about having earlier had such uncharitable thoughts concerning her sister.

Within moments of opening the envelope, however, Millie's dark mood had returned. There was no letter inside, only another Christmas card, containing the exact same message as the first.

Laura had obviously forgotten to cross Millie's name off the list after sending the first card and had sent a second by mistake. Unfortunately, the mistake showed precisely how generic and scripted the "personal" message was.

Millie took the first card out of its envelope and opened it next to the second card. She looked at them only long enough to confirm that they were the same, word for word. With a snort of disgust, she threw both cards into her kitchen junk drawer and slammed it shut.

It was bad enough that she hadn't seen her sister in years. It was bad enough that they only corresponded at Christmas and on their birthdays. But, if that correspondence had been reduced to a copy of the same insincere script that Laura sent to everyone on her mailing list, Millie didn't see the point of continuing it. She went to bed angry that night, unsure about whether she would bother to mail Laura a card in return.

But of course she did. Millie was a forgiving soul, and the next day, as she played an old cassette of her favorite carols, she wrote thoughtful, personal messages in cards for all of her friends and relatives. Laura remained on the list. Millie had decided that dealing with her hurt feelings in any other way would not be in keeping with the spirit of the season.

By four o'clock that afternoon, Millie had a tall stack of stamped, addressed envelopes and an advanced case of writer's cramp. Knowing that the only thing that would give her greater satisfaction than having the cards written would be to actually have them posted, she decided to warm up the truck and make the short drive to Darlene's store.

She found Darlene perched on her stool, chuckling over the stupidity of some game-show contestant.

"Lookit this," she said to Millie in place of a proper greeting. "This guy don't remember where his wife went to high school! Where do they find people so dumb, they don't even know their own relations?"

Millie shrugged and smiled. Then she handed Darlene the thick bundle of cards.

"Got a bunch of Christmas cards to mail," she said. "The top one's yours. I figured I could get away without a stamp on that one," she winked.

Darlene turned away from the television set.

"Oh, Millie! That's real nice of you, thanks." She took the envelope that had her name on it, placed it on the grimy counter and gave it a little pat with one doughy hand. She fed the rest of the cards two by two through the top slot of a locked bin that sat conveniently within arm's reach of the stool. "They'll go out tomorrow by 10," she assured Millie. "That's when Barry picks up the outgoing stuff."

Millie said "thank you" and turned to leave. Darlene stopped her before she opened the door.

"Oh! Hang on, there! I almost forgot, I got a card for you!" she said. When Millie came back to the counter, wearing an expectant smile, Darlene clarified what she had said.

"Not a card from *me*," she said, in an embarrassed tone. "I don't have all mine done up yet. I meant you got some mail from your sister. Another card, it looks like."

The smile slid off Millie's face and her eyes went to the mail cubbyholes.

"*Another* card?" she asked, incredulous.

"Looks like," Darlene grunted as she lifted her body off the stool and crossed the little patch of linoleum that defined her world. "Same sort of big envelope, anyway." She pulled the card out of Millie's mailbox and crossed back over to the counter. "Exact same," she commented as she handed it to Millie.

Exact same. Millie could see that it was, too. Same cool blue color, same neat, spidery handwriting, same snowflake sticker securing the flap at the back.

"Well, isn't that odd?" she said.

Darlene made some noncommittal noise. She was sneaking glances back at the game show she had been watching. They had just returned from a commercial break and were about to introduce another contestant who would leave Darlene feeling good about herself for the rest of the day. She used her little remote control to turn up the volume a bit and didn't even notice that Millie, who was normally very polite, left without remembering to say goodbye.

Millie didn't save the card for when she got home. She wanted to know what was inside the envelope, but didn't feel the same sort of delicious anticipation that she usually had about her personal mail. If anything, she felt

more of a nasty suspicion that she wished to either confirm or dispense with immediately. She tore the envelope
open the instant she was inside the cab of the truck. She
pulled out the card and opened it.

It was the same. Word for word, it was the same.

Millie's mental discomfort went up a notch. *How can
she be so forgetful?* she wondered. *What's wrong with her?*
With that unpleasant question lodged in her mind, Millie
put the truck into gear and started out for home.

Normally, Millie enjoyed driving through a winter sunset. She loved seeing the band of rich color on the horizon
and the long, cool shadows that the bare-branched trees
cast over the unbroken snow. She noticed none of it that
day, however, for she had begun to actively worry.

She and Laura had had an aunt who had been forgetful. That is, she had started out as simply forgetful, deteri-
orated into full-fledged feeble-mindedness and then died,
not knowing who she was or where she was. It had been
Alzheimer's, Millie supposed, but they had called it senil-
ity in those days. Their mother had told them not to be
too sad because their aunt had surely been happier than
she would have been had she been in her right mind.

Millie began doing the math. Their aunt had seemed
ancient to them at the time, but they had been children.
She supposed that the woman might have been in her 70s.
She herself was 62, which made Laura 65, come March.
Still young, really.

But it could age a person, having no support system and
no one to talk to except a mean, controlling husband. Millie
worried that it could nip away at a person, a little each day,
and make a body vulnerable to disease and deterioration.

"Stop it," she told herself, aloud. "Stop making a mountain out of a molehill." Laura had simply gotten a little out of control with the cards this year. She was no doubt stressed because she had to shop and bake and cook Christmas dinner for all her in-laws. It was no big thing. That is, it was not *necessarily* a big thing. Millie resolved that she would put the terrible thoughts out of her head, at least until she could examine all three cards objectively.

That evening, after clearing away her plate of barely touched leftover chicken and peas, Millie retrieved the first two cards from her kitchen junk drawer. She put them on the kitchen table, next to the identical third card, and sat down to have a really good look.

The message was exactly the same, word for word, pen stroke for pen stroke. The little haphazard dash that followed the *Dear Millie*, the odd angle of the exclamation point that followed Laura's wish for a merry Christmas, even the tiny flourish at the end of the signature—all had been perfectly duplicated. Millie saw that the notes had been written with the same precise margins and was sure that, had the card stock been transparent, she would have been able to stack the cards three deep and see the messages merge flawlessly together.

It was strange, it was puzzling but, in a way, it was a relief. The copies were too exact to have been produced by someone whose mind was slipping. Laura had done this deliberately, that much was apparent.

"But why?" Millie whispered, as she slid the cards back into their envelopes. "Why would you do such a thing, Laura?"

Millie had been gathering the envelopes up into a small stack when she noticed something else—something that made her drop the cards back on the tabletop.

It was the stamps. There were three envelopes and three stamps that had been stuck on identically askew. Beneath each crooked stamp was a dirty smudge, a bit of a thumbprint, Millie guessed. All three marks were the same. *Exactly the same.* Millie felt her small dinner turn to a cold lump in her stomach.

She's trying to tell me something, Millie thought. It was the only possible explanation. In her brief note, Laura had mentioned a "year of changes." *Could she be ready to leave him?* Millie wondered. *Does she want me to help?* She knew that Laura couldn't phone her, because the call would show up on her long-distance bill. But Millie could call Laura, in the morning, after Laura's husband had left for work.

"I'll do it; I'll call in the morning," Millie spoke the promise aloud, thinking that she would be more likely to keep it, if she did. Then she left the cards on the table and went to bed. She lay awake for quite some time, thinking about the things she might say to Laura. It had been more than 10 years since they had spoken. Millie smiled when she realized that the icy sensation of fear in her stomach had become a tingle of excitement.

Laura was looking well—*very* well. Her hair was the honey shade of blonde that it had been before she had begun dyeing it to hide the gray, and her skin was smooth and rosy. Millie was so happy to see her. There were a million things for them to talk about.

"Did you get my card?" Millie asked, even though she had only just mailed it.

"No," answered Laura. "I'm sorry, I don't get any mail. But it's so nice of you to send me a card when I never sent you one."

"But you sent me *three!*" Millie protested. "Tell me why you sent me so many cards—and all the same, too."

Laura smiled at Millie and began to walk away. Millie tried to follow but couldn't. She felt rooted in place.

"Little details," Laura called, over her shoulder. "Little details make all the difference."

And then, she was gone. Millie didn't feel alone, though. She looked to her right and saw Darlene, perched on her stool. Darlene was staring at her. She wore an expression of contempt.

"Where do they find people so dumb, they don't even know their own relations?" she said.

When Millie awoke, her pulse was thudding loudly in her ears and her nightgown was clinging to her skin in sweat-soaked patches. She threw on her old chenille robe, ran downstairs in a panic, picked up the telephone and fumbled through her address book for Laura's number. She dialed it without hesitation, even though it was the middle of the night and her brother-in-law was sure to be home.

Someone picked up halfway through the eighth ring.

"Who the hell is this?" said a deep, angry voice on the other end of the line.

Millie took a deep breath.

"Hello, Raymond," she said. "This is Millie. I apologize for calling at such a late hour, but I need to speak with Laura."

"It's two o'clock in the damn morning!" Raymond roared. "She's sleeping!"

"Yes, I know," Millie said, trying to sound stronger than she felt in the face of such intimidation. "I'm aware of the time, but it's urgent. Would you wake her, please?"

There was a pause. Millie imagined that Raymond was trying to decide whether he should hang up or satisfy his curiosity.

"Look," he said, "why don't you tell me what you gotta tell her and I'll pass it on in the morning."

Millie held her ground.

"I'm worried about her," she said. "I need to speak with her, right now, to know she's alright."

"She's *fine*," Raymond thundered. "She'll stay fine, as long as you don't call here again, meddling! She sent you a damn Christmas card, didn't she?"

Raymond slammed the phone down, leaving Millie listening to the hollow sound of a dead line and the competing voices that were playing in her mind.

Little details make all the difference...

She sent you a damn Christmas card, didn't she?...

"No," Millie said, softly, as she placed the phone receiver back in its cradle. "I don't think she did."

She walked over to the kitchen table, where she had left the three cards. She spread them out again and found the little detail that she was looking for. The postmarks on all three cards were the same. They were positioned alike, the ink was faded in the same places and dark in the same places, and they all gave the same date: December ninth. Millie had received the cards on three different days but, really, they were one card, mailed on one day, by someone who was careless about whether their hands were dirty or the stamps went on straight.

And that wouldn't be Laura.

Millie knew that as well as she knew her own name. Laura had written her Christmas cards, she had addressed them, but, for some reason, Raymond had mailed them. And Millie suddenly knew, with stone-cold certainty, that she would keep receiving the same card, again and again, until she knew what that reason was.

Millie didn't go back to bed that night. She sat at the table with a notepad and a pen until she had come up with a story to tell the police. She needed them to take her seriously and she couldn't tell the truth without sounding like a crazy lady. Millie had fabricated a plausible cause for concern and made her call to a police precinct in Laura's city by 7 AM.

A somber-sounding detective called her back before noon.

Later on, the detective told Millie that they might never have had enough evidence to charge Raymond had she not called when she did.

"He was being very thorough," he said. "We could see that he had been systematically been disposing of all the evidence—the weapon, the...um..."

"Her body," Millie said. She was past the shock of it at that point. She had reached the point where she could talk about her murdered sister in plain terms.

An hour later, as she watched the detective turn from the snowy lane to the main road on his way back to the city, Millie realized that she might also be past the point of crying at the mere sight of the Christmas cards. Though the holidays were over—they had passed in a strange fog of pain and disbelief—she thought it might be nice to give all three of the cards their moment of being displayed on the mantle.

But it was the strangest thing. When Millie opened the kitchen drawer where she had been keeping the cards, she could find only one of the three. And, although there was no way of knowing, she *did* know, without a doubt, that it was the first card. The first card—which had been written by her sister and mailed by her sister's monstrous husband in an effort to maintain appearances. It had worked; Millie had to admit that it had worked at first.

"But I caught on eventually, didn't I, Laura?"

Millie set the card on the mantle and sat down where she could look at it while she remembered how beautiful Laura had been the last time she saw her.

"Oooh! Millie! Hold up—you got some mail, here." Darlene banged on the counter with a meaty hand to get Millie's attention and stop her from leaving the store. She shuffled over to the mailboxes, where she paused, with a confused look on her face.

"I'll be damned," she said, as her eyes scanned the mostly empty cubbyholes. "I didn't already give it to you, did I?"

"Give me what?" Millie asked. She stood with her purse in one hand and her little bag of purchases in the other, waiting to go.

"The mail from your sister. I swear I saw it because, I was thinking that it must've got lost somewheres in the post office. That she must've mailed it just *before*. Terrible thing. It looked like another one of those big, blue Christmas cards."

Millie smiled and waved to Darlene as she headed back toward the door.

"That's okay," she said. "Don't worry about it, Darlene. I know what it was; it wasn't a Christmas card."

And before Darlene could ask any questions that Millie didn't care to answer, Millie was outside and the bell was clanging loudly as the weathered old door banged shut behind her.

"It was a 'thank you' card," Millie whispered to herself. Then she climbed into her truck and aimed it for home, feeling rather relieved that there would be no mail to read when she got there.

Betty's Butter Tarts

It was tradition. Every Christmas, the ladies of Mardale County got together at the drafty old community hall by the gravel crossroads and put on the Mardale County Ladies Christmas Bake Sale. Everyone would come from miles around, ostensibly because the proceeds went to charity. Truth be told, however, it was because the Mardale County Ladies really knew how to bake.

For an entire Saturday, the community hall would be filled with the most tempting sights and mouth-watering aromas. There were golden pies, filled to bursting with blueberries or cherries that had been canned the previous summer or with apples that had been generously sprinkled with cinnamon and sugar. There were cookies—fancy ones like pinwheels, lemon-drops and cherry-almond buttons, and traditional Christmas ones like buttery shortbread and fragrant gingersnaps. There were marvelously chewy squares made with dates and nuts and sweet flakes of snowy coconut, and there were hand-dipped chocolates with centers of luscious fondant. There were fruitcakes, of course, both light and dark, soaked in rum and topped with creamy almond paste. There were aromatic sweet rolls, gooey and sticky and laden with cream cheese icing. And then there were Betty's butter tarts.

Every year, Betty Rumbold filled two big, folding tables with trays of what many referred to as "the most delectable edible this side of heaven." They were so spectacular that if, in July, someone spoke the phrase "Betty's butter tarts," it would conjure sensory memories sufficient to set anyone's mouth salivating. Betty was always sold out one hour after the Mardale County Ladies had unlocked the doors of the hall. One year, when she broke her arm and could only bake enough to fill one table, there was great disappointment in general and a passionate fistfight over the last half-dozen cellophane-wrapped tarts. When people spoke of that year, they spoke with great solemnity. They said that Christmas just hadn't seemed the same.

Those who failed to understand the worship that Betty's butter tarts commanded were those who, for some reason or another, had never had the opportunity to sample one. Anyone who had tasted them knew that they were magical indeed.

The pastry shells were tender, flaky and baked to golden perfection. Each one was brimming with a filling made of raisins that had been soaked in thick maple syrup until they were plump to the point of bursting and then folded into a buttery, creamy, brown sugar mixture. There was a hint of something else—some said brandy, some said rum—that gave the tarts a lingering aftertaste that was more complex than that of a purely sweet treat. And there was something about Betty's technique, of course, that made the confections impossible to duplicate. Most of the ladies knew that, because most of them had tried to do it. But Betty's recipe was Betty's carefully guarded secret. It had been given to her by her mother, who had received it from her grandmother, who had received it from her great-grandmother, and so on. What most people found disturbing about this matriarchal tradition was the fact that Betty Rumbold had no daughter of her own.

She had a son. He was a gangly sort of big fellow called Buddy, who showed no interest in baked goods aside from the consumption of them. He was shy, awkward and not particularly promising in terms of marriage either, so it seemed unlikely that Betty would even get herself a daughter-in-law to whom she could pass the recipe. This caused great concern in the community—there was great worry that Betty would someday die and take her fabulous butter tart recipe to the grave.

"I have no intention of dying just yet," she would say whenever the subject was raised. But, of course, intentions have little to do with the way life turns out. Betty did die, quite unexpectedly one year, and the entire county turned out at her funeral. Together, everyone mourned the simultaneous losses of a good woman and an exemplary butter tart.

The following two Christmases were difficult for everyone. The Mardale County Ladies went on with their annual bake sale, of course, and raised great sums of money for whatever charity they were in support of. People bought the pies, cakes and cookies that were offered for sale and found them all to be fine. But what could not be hidden beneath an extra dusting of confectioner's sugar was the fact that everyone missed Betty's butter tarts.

Of course, to simply say "missed" might be understating it the tiniest bit.

There were those who literally dreamed of the treats. Night after night, their sleep would be disrupted by images of delightful, sweet tarts that were always just beyond their reach. Others who suffered from seasonally induced cravings overate terribly, stuffing their faces from morning until night in search of the ever-elusive taste. The search for relief included many efforts to popularize new and different butter tart recipes—but all the variations that were tried turned out to be crushing disappointments. It would be fair to say that, while Christmas was still celebrated in Mardale County, it was done in an atmosphere of real suffering.

Fortunately, several months before the Christmas bake sale on the third year after Betty's untimely death, her ghost appeared. There was tremendous excitement when a frizzy-headed young woman named Bernice came forward to announce that Betty had come to her as a shimmering wraith and had delivered the message that she was prepared to pass on her recipe for butter tarts.

"So what is it, then?" everyone wanted to know.

Bernice twisted a wild tendril of hair around one finger and shrugged.

"She didn't get that *specific*," the girl explained. "She said I could get it from her kid."

At the urging of everyone who knew her, Bernice made an inquiring phone call to Buddy Rumbold, who was of no assistance whatsoever. Not knowing what else to do, Bernice decided that she would simply sit around and wait for a further sign from the spirit of Betty Rumbold.

Betty did appear again, one week later, but not to the lazy Bernice. Her shifting, vaporous shape materialized in front of a skinny, blonde waitress named Beryl, causing her to drop her tray of club sandwiches and meatloaf specials. Everyone was quite angry until she told them what had happened.

"She was sort of glowing, you know, and see-through, but it was Betty, all right. And she says to me, she says, 'I am seeking a young woman worthy of my butter tart

Beryl explained
to the engrossed lunch crowd. Then Beryl hung up her
apron, took the afternoon off and went out to the
Rumbold farm in person to claim her prize.

"I'll tell you what I told that other girl," Buddy sighed
when Beryl knocked on his door and demanded to be
given his mother's secret recipe. "I don't know where it is."

Beryl and Buddy shared a bit of an unpleasant exchange.
Finally, she stormed off, stomping as dramatically as she
could with her skinny little legs and her puny feet.

"Betty Rumbold is *still* hogging that recipe," she told
her customers, afterward. "She's hoggin' it all the way
from the great beyond."

Week after week, Betty's luminous form appeared.
Each time, she delivered the same message—but to a different girl. Each time, the girl would call up Buddy or pay
him a visit, wanting to be given the butter tart secret.
None met with any success.

One week, Betty floated into the Mardale County
library and spoke with a quiet, rather mousy clerk named
Bonnie.

Bonnie said nothing to her co-workers of the
encounter, but at the end of the day, she put on her coat,
climbed into her beat-up old car and drove out of town to
visit Buddy Rumbold.

"Not again," he said when he answered the door.

"I am sorry to bother you," Bonnie apologized. "I
know that you've been a bit under siege, lately, as it were.
It's just that it seemed so important to your mother. I
thought I should at least come by and let you know that
she appeared to me."

Buddy softened a bit.

"Yeah, well, I appreciate that and all," he said. "I just don't know what to do about it. I honestly don't know where Mum kept the recipe and I'm not sure that I'd recognize it even if I *did* find it. It's a real problem. Every week, I'm getting pestered by some horrible new girl. Present company excluded," he added hastily. "You don't seem that bad."

"Well," said Bonnie, as she raised an eyebrow, "I suppose I could help you look for the recipe. Once you find it, you can give it away and be free of all the bother."

Buddy thought that sounded sensible. He invited Bonnie in and the two of them conducted a systematic search of the kitchen. They pored over Betty's cookbooks and rifled through her index cards and scanned every yellowing bit of paper that she had ever tucked away into her recipe scrapbook. They found nothing and eventually had to give up out of sheer weariness.

"Boy," Buddy said, as he rubbed at his tired eyes, "lookin' through all of this reminds me what a good cook Mum was. I mostly microwave things these days."

Bonnie smiled as she put the last of the binders away.

"Well, I'm not the cook that your mother was," she said, "but I could make us a little supper before I leave. I wouldn't mind at all."

Buddy accepted, Bonnie cooked and the two spent a very pleasant evening together.

The next week, Buddy Rumbold was surprised to see Bonnie on his doorstep once more.

"It's odd," he said, as he rubbed his chin thoughtfully. "She's never appeared to anyone more'n one time before."

Bonnie shook her head innocently.

"She was very insistent that we keep searching," she said. "*Very* insistent."

And, so, Buddy invited Bonnie inside. The two of them went through cupboards and shelves and tore out the lavender paper that lined the drawers of what had been Betty Rumbold's bureau. They examined every corner of every closet until they were exhausted. Then they sat down together, shared a meal and shook their heads over what a waste of time it had been.

But, in fact, when it was time to say goodnight, neither one of them felt much as though they had wasted an evening. Bonnie sang along with the radio all the way home, while Buddy cheerfully washed up the dishes. Both went to sleep that night thinking of things other than pastry.

And so it continued for several more weeks. Truth be told, there wasn't much recipe hunting that went on after Bonnie's second visit, but the two young people got on so famously that neither one gave it a thought. And, if Betty Rumbold's specter was upset that the search was being neglected, she didn't show it. There were no further sightings of her reported by anyone.

After a suitable period of time, Buddy got up the nerve to ask Bonnie to marry him. She got up the nerve to say yes, and the two tied the knot. On their wedding night, as they reminisced about the strange way they had met, Buddy grew serious.

"It's too bad we never found that recipe," he said. "Mum would have wanted you to have it."

Bonnie smiled and cupped her new husband's face in her hands.

"I found something better," she said, and she kissed him to show that she meant it.

One week later, Buddy and Bonnie Rumbold arrived home from their honeymoon. As Bonnie walked into the kitchen of what had become her house as well as Buddy's, she spied a white square of paper sitting in the middle of the dinette table.

"Buddy," she said. "What's this?"

That year, for the first time in three years, someone booked a double table for the Mardale County Ladies Christmas Bake Sale. When Bonnie Rumbold arrived and set to work filling both of those tables with trays upon trays of glistening, golden butter tarts, everyone was very pleased.

Of course, to simply say "pleased" might be understating it the tiniest bit.

People had lined up clear across the hall, through the double doors, down the stairs and out to the gravel crossroads. The luscious tarts sold within a half-hour of the first customer taking the first bite and declaring gleefully, "It's them! It's them!" The other ladies sold their baked treats eventually, but only after the last syrupy morsel of the last delectable butter tart was licked from the last finger.

"Incredible," sighed one man, as he let out his belt a notch. "That Betty Rumbold sure did set the baking standard."

Everyone agreed that it was true. But, interestingly, it was the last time Betty's name was spoken in that exact context. Every Christmas thereafter, people scrambled to buy "Bonnie's butter tarts."

In the strangest of ways, from the greatest of distances, the pastry torch, it seemed, had been passed.

Coco's Christmas Present

There once was an elderly woman named Hazel who lived in a terrible, run-down neighborhood with her little dog, whom she called "Coco." The neighborhood hadn't always been in an awful state; it had actually been quite lovely and well-kept when Hazel and her husband had first taken the apartment there. But slowly, over many years, it had declined. The good neighbors eventually moved away to safer or more prestigious addresses, and the low rents attracted less desirable tenants. Hazel might have moved, but then her husband died and too many changes at one time seemed to her to be a bad idea. So she stayed. She kept her own pretty window boxes neatly tended, painted her own kitchen when the walls began to look dull and kept her own little apartment very well, despite the dirt and disrepair that she saw every time she stepped outside of it. And when the unpleasant noises of the neighborhood began to frighten her at night, she went looking for some reassuring company. She found it in the small bundle of brown fur that was Coco.

Coco might have had a little terrier in her and she might have had a little dachshund. The people at the animal shelter couldn't say for sure, but Hazel didn't care one bit about the lack of pedigree. Coco had big, liquid eyes and a warm, pink tongue and was as gentle and affectionate as any pet could be. The two got on very well, and from that day forward, when Hazel heard angry voices in the hallway or drunken parties in the apartment above her or fistfights outside her bedroom window, she didn't worry so much. With Coco's warm little body snuggled beside her, she felt quite secure indeed.

In return for her affection and companionship, Hazel pampered Coco in any way that she was able to. She kept her fur neatly clipped when the weather was hot and knit smart little sweaters for her to wear when the winter winds blew. Coco shared Hazel's bed at night and had a luxurious velvet pillow of her own to lounge upon during the day. She ate the tastiest morsels from the chops and chickens that Hazel fried and lapped her water out of a beautiful little cut-glass bowl. She was treated as well as a human person every day of the year—including special occasions.

On Valentine's Day, Hazel always found a card with lovely red hearts and some appropriately sentimental message of "puppy love." For Easter, she hid little doggy treats around the apartment so Coco could enjoy something akin to an egg hunt. Hazel made clever costumes for Coco every Halloween, fed her bits of turkey on Thanksgiving and wrapped up a special gift for her to open each Christmas morning. She knew that the little dog appreciated it all. She could tell by her cheerfully sharp little barks and the excited way she would lick at Hazel's hand.

One December day, very close to Christmas, Hazel put on her warm wool coat and the fancy scarf that she only ever wore when she was going uptown on the bus. As she tied the laces of her sturdy, fleece-lined boots, Coco began to circle her feet expectantly.

"Not this time, Coco," Hazel said as she pulled on her gloves. "I'm going on a very special shopping trip today."

Coco whimpered her disappointment and Hazel felt guilty—but only a little. She couldn't take Coco with her because she was going out to buy Coco's Christmas gift.

It would ruin the surprise entirely if she saw it being purchased, and Hazel knew that Coco loved the surprise as much as the gift itself. So she kissed her pet on the top of her fuzzy, chocolate-colored head, locked the door and set out on her shopping trip.

It was a lovely day to be buying a Christmas gift. The windows of all the stores had wonderful displays in them and the streets were bright and beautiful with holiday decorations. Droves of people had ventured out to shop. Some were too hurried and tended to be a little cranky because of it, but most were more cheerful than they would be if you found yourself in a lineup with them at any other time of the year. Hazel enjoyed herself immensely. She chatted with the clerks whenever she met one who wasn't being rushed off his or her feet, and she stopped mid-afternoon to treat herself to a cup of tea and a bacon-and-tomato sandwich at a cafeteria. She browsed through dozens of shops before she finally settled on a gift for Coco: a cunning little stuffed cat. It had a bell sewn to its collar, so it was perfect for shaking, and it was fashioned out of rawhide, so it was perfect for chewing. Hazel was pleased as she could be. She tucked her special purchase into her handbag and made her way back to the bus stop.

She arrived just in time to see her bus roaring off down the street. Hazel wasn't bothered; she was a patient woman and was in no great hurry. But, as she waited for the next bus in her patient way, she saw that the light was quickly fading from the sky. She had been having such a grand time in the stores that she hadn't paid attention to the time. It was late—at least later than usual for Hazel to be out—and

she was anxious to be home with her door securely locked and a nice bit of supper cooking on the stove.

Another bus finally came along and Hazel was happily on her way. She passed the time on the rather long ride by thinking about the comfortably familiar things that she would do once she arrived home. Coco would be *very* hungry; feeding her something tasty would be first on Hazel's agenda. Then she'd make a meal for herself while she teased the little dog with vague hints about her Christmas gift.

"Coco," she might say, "I've been thinking that it's time you had a little four-legged friend." Or, "Coco, wouldn't you like a present that you can really sink your teeth into?"

Hazel was no clever conversationalist. She knew that, but it didn't bother her for she also knew that Coco didn't care a bit.

By the time Hazel arrived at the bus stop that was a little more than a block away from her building, darkness had fallen. The darkness was not interrupted by the cheerful twinkling of Christmas lights or the glitter of holiday decorations. No one who lived near Hazel made that kind of effort anymore. Her neighborhood had become one that was seamy in the daylight hours and genuinely unnerving at night.

Hazel dreaded the thought of walking unescorted along the street, but she did what she could to appear street smart and brave. She tucked her bag inside her coat, drew herself up to her full height and stepped along smartly. She cut a less than intimidating figure but did her best to not look like a potential victim. The effort seemed to pay off. The trio of teenagers leaning against the barred windows of the pawnshop and smoking let her pass with no more than a casual "better get home, Grandma," and the tough girls shivering on the corner in their leather minis and fake fur bomber jackets said nothing to her at all. Hazel could hear footsteps fall in behind her at one point, and her heart began to race nervously. Whoever it was stopped following when she passed the liquor store, though; she could hear the tinkling of the bell as the door was pulled open.

When she finally turned her key in the front door of her apartment building, Hazel breathed a deep sigh of relief. She scolded herself for having been foolish and resolved to never again be so unmindful of the time. Then she trudged wearily up the half-dozen steps that led to her floor.

Hazel's apartment was at the far end of the hallway, but she could clearly see her door from the top of the stairs. On this particular night, she could clearly see that her door was *open*. She stopped in her tracks, wondering why that would be and what she should do about it. But before any answers could come to her, Coco did. The little dog came tearing out of the apartment and down the long, filthy, threadbare carpet that lined the hall.

She was snarling and baring her teeth like a wild animal.

"Coco!" Hazel said, thinking that the sound of her voice would calm the dog. But it didn't. Coco's lips remained tightly drawn back, the hair on her back and neck still bristled, and the glint in her usually loving eyes was vicious.

"Coco, stop!" Hazel ordered. But Coco didn't stop and Hazel realized that she had about a second to get herself out of harm's way. She turned and fled back down the stairs as quickly as her old legs would permit and yanked open the heavy front door. Once she was outside, she slammed it shut behind her. As she stood, catching her breath, beneath the burned-out lamp that hung over the door, Hazel could hear that Coco was still barking madly inside. When she turned around and looked through the small security window, she could see her little pet standing guard at the top of the stairs. When the dog's brown eyes met Hazel's, they narrowed menacingly. Her hackles raised up once more, and from the way her black lips were quivering, Hazel could tell that she was growling.

Hazel had always considered herself a capable person. When a problem arose, she could usually tell what had to be done and would do it. As she stood on the crumbling front stoop of her building door on that night, however—afraid to be outside and afraid to go inside, confused by the attack of her beloved pet and worried about the fact that the door to her apartment stood mysteriously open—she was truly bewildered. She stood for quite a long time, trying to decide upon a course of action. Finally, the sound of drunken voices across the street reminded her that she would do well to get herself inside. Coco was still threatening her from the top of the stairs, but the building had a back door. Hazel thought that she could sneak in that way, tiptoe down to the superintendent's apartment and see if he could be of some help.

Unless, of course, he was already in her apartment.

The thought occurred to Hazel as she was following the cracked, uneven sidewalk that led around the side of the building, and it filled her with relief. Suddenly, the whole confusing, frightening situation made sense. For weeks, she had been complaining that her kitchen faucet was dripping. The superintendent, a lazy fellow who always stank of something stale and unpleasant, had obviously worked up the ambition to take care of the leak— but, in doing so, had frightened Coco and let her out of the apartment. That was an annoyance and it was a problem, but it was far from insurmountable.

When Hazel reached the back door, she already held her key in her gloved hand. One look at the lock told her that she didn't need it, though. It was broken again; the works of it were hanging from the door like a metal eyeball dangling from its socket. Hazel clucked her tongue and shook her head and pulled the door open to let herself in.

She was careful to be very quiet. Hazel thought that if she didn't alarm Coco further, she could slip down the superintendent's apartment and sit with his equally slothful wife until the faucet was fixed. Then she could return to her own place and calm the little dog in surroundings that were familiar to them both. All she had to do was sneak in...

But then Coco was there, racing down the stairs toward Hazel and snarling savagely. Hazel let out an involuntary shriek and ran. She ran down the stairs and down the hall, past the doors of the cheap basement suites. She didn't stop by the superintendent's apartment; she knew that she didn't have time to knock politely on the door to see if his wife was at home. Instead, she took refuge in the laundry room at the end of the hall, slamming the door shut to protect her from Coco's fiercely snapping teeth.

The door to the laundry room had a window from which a person could stare down the length of the hallway and up the short flight of stairs leading to the back door. The glass had been broken for longer than Hazel could remember, but it didn't much matter. The window was high enough that Hazel had to stand on her toes in order to peek through it; it was certainly too high for Coco to jump through, no matter how rabid her mood.

For a few moments, Hazel sagged against the door, catching her breath and listening to Coco pace in the hall. The basement floor was covered in faded green linoleum instead of carpet, and the little dog's toenails clicked rhythmically on its surface. Hazel could tell by the sound that Coco was walking around in circles, though, not walking away. When she raised up on tiptoes and peered through the window, she saw that she was right. Coco was guarding the door, stalking back and forth, making sure that her mistress could not escape.

"Coco, what's gotten into you?" Hazel said.

The dog looked up at the window and growled threateningly. Whatever had gotten into her didn't look like it was going to get out in a hurry, so Hazel slumped down on the grimy bench where people sat while they were sorting their colors from their whites and tried to think of what to do next.

It was then that she heard the voices.

"Go, man, get out of here!" said one.

"We didn't close the door," said the other.

"Who the hell cares?" the first voice shouted. "Let's *move!*"

Hazel jumped up from the bench and looked out the window just in time to see two men in dirty blue jeans and denim jackets running out the back door. They were carrying armloads of things. A long, black, electrical cord dragged along like a tail behind the second man as he ran. Hazel didn't need anyone to tell her that the other end of that cord connected to the new portable stereo that she used to listen to her Guy Lombardo cassettes.

At the very same moment when she understood that she had been robbed, Hazel also understood Coco's bizarre behavior. The little dog hadn't been attacking her; she had been *herding* her out of harm's way.

As the heavy rear door slammed shut behind the two thieves, Coco's demeanor changed. She turned and looked up at Hazel, who was still peering cautiously through the window. The violent gleam had left her eyes. She whimpered apologetically and scratched her nose with one front paw. The ferocity was gone. She still paced in circles, but did so eagerly, as she waited for her mistress to come out of the laundry room.

"Oh, Coco!" Hazel said as she hurried out into the hall. "Did they frighten you? Are you alright?"

Coco panted happily and licked once at Hazel's gloved hand. For years afterward, Hazel would wonder whether she would have actually felt her pet's small, wet tongue had she not been wearing those gloves. She wondered because of the unfathomable thing that had happened next.

Coco had turned around, scampered down the hallway and vanished.

Her fur is ruffled, Hazel thought at first when she noticed that Coco appeared to be a little blurred around the edges. *I need my glasses,* she told herself when the image of the little dog began to shimmer like a mirage. By the time Coco had gone half the length of the hallway, though, she had taken on an appearance that could not be explained away by ruffled fur or poor vision or any other natural means: she was transparent. Within a few more steps, she had faded from sight altogether. A moment or so after that, the clicking sound of her toenails disappeared as well. Hazel was left alone in the hallway, astonished at what she had seen and terrified of what she would see when she went upstairs to inspect her freshly burgled apartment.

The stereo had been taken, of course, as well as the clock radio and an expensive set of kitchen knives. The sugar bowl where Hazel collected spare change lay in pieces in the sink and had been emptied of all but a few pennies. The antique jewelry box was missing from the top of the dresser—along with the two emergency 50-dollar bills and half-dozen pieces of real jewelry that it contained. In every room, most things that hadn't been taken had been destroyed by the robbers. Hazel wept at each terrible discovery, but at none so much as the horrible find that she made in the bathroom. There, crumpled in the bottom of the tub with her head at an odd angle lay Coco. Her little, pink tongue lolled out of her mouth, but it no longer looked as though it would feel warm and moist on the back of a person's hand.

"Coco," cried Hazel, and she reached out a trembling hand to pet her small friend. Eventually, because she could think of nothing else to say, she told the still, little dog, "I got you a nice Christmas present."

Coco didn't answer. She didn't bark her excited little bark and she didn't wag her tail.

It took another half hour before Hazel was willing to accept that she never again would.

The very next day, Hazel dried her puffy, red eyes and went out looking for another apartment. She found one, in a nice complex where there were properly locking front and back doors and yard lamps that cast their revealing lights out in wide arcs over the grounds at night. Not that they even seemed necessary, for it was a better neighborhood, in every sense. Hazel saw wreaths hanging on the doors and Christmas lights draped on the evergreen trees and imagined that she would feel quite safe walking about there after dark.

Hazel spent all the rest of the days leading up to Christmas packing her belongings. When Christmas morning arrived, however, she neither packed nor treated herself to a day of leisure. Instead, she tucked a small package into her large handbag, put on her good scarf and her warm, wool coat and set out walking in the fresh snow.

After a few blocks, Hazel walked into a vacant lot that was surrounded by a sagging, chain-link fence. A few people had gone to the trouble of erecting a swing set there. Some others had planted a half-dozen small trees. Bit by bit, the barren space had been converted into a makeshift park where neighborhood children could play. It had been a place where Coco had liked to play, too. Hazel liked to think that her spirit had settled there, where she could run with the children every day and nap on the lawn come summer.

There was a picnic table in the corner of the park, where Hazel had spent many hours watching Coco chase her tail and dig craters in the sandbox. She made her way over to the table, brushed the snow off one of the long bench seats and sat down. Then she opened her handbag and took out the package, which she had wrapped in colorful paper and tied with satin ribbon.

"Merry Christmas, Coco," she said, although no one was there to hear her. "I don't know if you're here, but I think you might be. And I wanted to say 'thank you' to you, for what you did. You always took such good care of me. It's going to be hard, but now I'll just have to take good care of myself.

"Anyway," she continued, "I brought you something. You'll like it, I think. It's a Christmas present!"

Hazel turned and swept a bit of snow off the table. She set the package down on the spot she had cleared and gave it a little pat.

"Here you go, Coco," she said. Hazel was silent for several moments and had to clear her throat before she could continue.

"I wanted to make sure you got your present," she explained, "because you already gave me mine."

Hazel patted the colorfully wrapped gift once more, then stood up and walked away. She went home and managed to finish most of her packing that day, despite having to stop every few minutes to wipe at her eyes.

A few days later, as she rode past the park in a taxicab that was taking her to her new home, she saw that the package was gone. She knew that anyone could have taken it and supposed that someone had. In her heart, though, she hoped that the bright paper had been shredded by small sharp teeth and that the ribbon had been enthusiastically batted about by little paws.

She hoped that, wherever she was, Coco had received her Christmas present.

The Mistletoe

Once upon a time many years ago, a young couple began their married life. They had each other, great hope for the future and a decent little piece of land to farm. What they did not have much of was money. For the most part, they were content enough to make do with what they had, but as they neared their first Christmas together, the man could see that his young wife was tired of being poor.

Each day, he tried some little way to cheer her. Nothing he did seemed to help, although she noticed and appreciated his efforts.

"Don't mind me," the young farm wife finally told her husband on Christmas Eve. "I'm only a little sad that on our first Christmas as husband and wife we aren't able to give each other any gifts."

The husband promised that the next year would be better, but his wife's discontent weighed heavily on his mind and heart. Late that night, while she slept, he lay awake and worried.

At one point, he had an idea. Quietly, the young husband slipped out of the bedroom and tiptoed downstairs to the corner by the old cast-iron stove where his wife kept her sewing basket. He found several scraps of soft, green felt and some buttons and beads that looked like ripe berries. He took out scissors, a needle and thread and set about making a Christmas morning surprise.

He wasn't accustomed to sewing and it wasn't easy. He stabbed himself three times with the needle and accidentally looped one stitch through his baggy long johns. In the end, however, he was pleased with the result. He turned down the lamp, returned to the comfort of his bed and waited for Christmas morning to arrive.

When it did, a few hours later, he told his wife to stay warm under the covers.

"I have something for you," he said. "Wait here for a few minutes."

When he walked back into the room, he was carrying a cup of hot tea and a thick slice of fried bread sprinkled with sugar.

"That was very sweet of you," she said when she had finished her little breakfast. "It was a lovely gift."

"That's not all," boasted the husband. "I have something else."

From behind his back, he produced his lumpy sewing craft. He held it between the thumb and forefinger of his right hand and dangled it above his wife's head. Though it was crudely made, she could see that it was meant to be a leafy sprig of mistletoe.

Before she could comment, he kissed her. It was a very long, soft, sweet kiss that left the young wife's lips tingling. Then, before she was even able to catch her breath, the husband pressed the homemade ornament into his wife's hand and spoke very seriously.

"There will be Christmases when we are rich and Christmases when we are poor," he said. "There will be years when there are gifts under the tree and years when the tree itself is hard to come by. But none of that will matter as long as we have each other. I made this to always remind us that we've already been given the greatest gift."

The young wife smiled at her husband. Her eyes were shining with tears.

"You're right," she said. "I'll always remember."
And she always did.

The young couple worked hard and over time the little farm flourished. Each Christmas, there were a few more special treats on the table and a few more gifts beneath the pretty tree. It wasn't long before there were babies, too—a chubby, laughing boy and a serious, bright little girl—who made the holidays even more complete. The children loved their Christmas Day surprises, as all children do, but they grew up knowing that there were more important things. They knew because every year their parents would bring out the scrappy-looking little mistletoe decoration, share a kiss beneath it and tell their son and daughter that having a loving family was the greatest gift of all.

Eventually, the son and daughter grew up and left home. They found their own soul mates, started their own families and had their own homes—sometimes far away from the farm where they had grown up. Almost every year they gathered at the farm for Christmas. They told their parents—whom everyone now called "Gran" and "Grandad"—that it was hard to imagine spending the holidays anywhere else.

"It's so much prettier here," the daughter often said as she gazed out over the snowy fields, watching the sun melt into the horizon.

"The kids have such fun here," the son would announce as he herded a crowd of rosy-faced children into the creaky old horse-drawn sleigh for an afternoon ride.

"And we're all family here," Gran would say. "That's all you need to make a good Christmas, remember?"

No one was likely to forget. They had Gran, Grandad and the beloved, ragged little piece of mistletoe to remind them.

Then one very sad year, Grandad died.

It happened in the summertime; his heart stopped beating on a humid day as he was painting the garage. Months later, as the holidays approached, everyone quietly agreed that Gran was not yet herself and that it would be a good idea to arrive a little earlier than usual for Christmas to help with the preparations.

The son and his wife came with a carload of groceries and immediately got down to the business of baking treats and planning the big Christmas meal.

The daughter and her husband made up beds and sofas for everyone who was staying and wrapped the few gifts that Gran had bothered to buy. Then they put up the tree that had been tied to the roof of their car since they had left the city and pulled the old box of Christmas ornaments out of the attic.

"Do you want to help decorate, Gran?" one of the teenage grandchildren asked.

"No, sweetheart. I'll just watch," answered Gran, who had been listlessly watching all the events of the day.

The tinsel, baubles and strands of twinkling lights were all hung with care. A number of other ornaments were placed upon the polished oak mantle and on the small end tables. A bushy wreath, dotted with red velvet ribbons, was placed on the front door. Then the daughter gathered up all the containers and extra bits and pieces and stuffed every-thing back into the large cardboard carton. She was about to return the box to the attic when her mother stopped her.

"Where's the mistletoe?" the older woman asked.

The daughter reddened a little. She had thought it best to discreetly forget about the mistletoe on this particular year. She had thought that Gran would not want to be reminded of the fact that she would not be getting her special Christmas kiss from Grandad.

"I forgot, Mom," was all the daughter said.

"How could you forget! Not one of these things that you're so busy doing is half as important as that little piece of mistletoe and what it stands for!" Gran had stood up to make her little speech. There were patches of hectic color in her cheeks.

The daughter quickly made amends.

"I'm sorry," she said. "You're right, of course. I'll hang it up now."

The worn, frayed, little decoration was hung in its usual place in the front hallway. Everyone shared their kisses and hugs beneath it, and Gran told them the story that they all knew, of how the mistletoe had been made by Grandad so many years before to remind them that they had already been given the greatest of gifts.

The next night was Christmas Eve. Because it was the first Christmas Eve without her father, the daughter found it difficult to sleep.

Warm milk will help, she thought. She slipped into her robe, snuck out of the spare room that she was sharing with her husband and quietly made her way downstairs to the kitchen.

She had just taken a mug down from the shelf when something shining in her peripheral vision captured her attention. The daughter turned in time to see a strange, eerie light pulsing down the hallway. It wasn't the reliable, dull, yellow glow of her mother's reading lamp or the sharp glare of the overhead fluorescent bulb in the laundry room. This was shimmering and warm, and it ebbed and flowed like a radiant tide. It was mysterious and it begged investigation.

The daughter set her mug on the countertop and tentatively approached the archway where the kitchen turned into the hall. Her eyes searched for the source of the glow and found it at the far end of the hall—in the entranceway, in the place where the mistletoe was hung. In the place where she could see her mother, standing beneath the mistletoe.

Gran's eyes were closed and she was swaying ever so slightly but was clearly in no danger of falling. As the daughter stood and watched, she could see the light—the swirling, flickering light—encircling and supporting her mother. At one point, Gran tilted her head back gently and pursed her lips. The light intensified for a moment; it seemed to draw itself together and concentrate into a form that was nearly opaque.

And then, very suddenly, it was gone.

Gran was smiling slightly, and she raised her hand to gently touch her fingers to her lips. The daughter, sensing that she had witnessed something quite private, quickly withdrew into the shadows of the kitchen. She busied herself making her cup of warm milk, and by the time she had finished, the hallway was dark and deserted once more.

By Christmas morning, the daughter was beginning to doubt what she had seen. It seemed so strange, she would easily have convinced herself that she had been dreaming had it not been for the significant change she noticed in her mother. Others noticed as well.

"Mom seems to be herself again," the son smiled as he watched Gran laughing with her grandchildren.

The daughter agreed but stopped short of telling her brother what she believed it was that had brought about the change.

There were several more happy Christmases at the farm, and the mistletoe—nearly falling apart on account of its age—presided over them all. Then there came a subdued holiday season when Gran had a pale, drawn look about her and admitted that she wasn't feeling well. Before the next Christmas came, she was gone.

The son and daughter took their families out to the farm that year anyway. It was partly out of tradition and partly because there was business to discuss. Gran had left the farm to her children, who needed to agree upon what was to be done with it.

The daughter felt strongly that the property should stay in the family.

The son, with two kids in college, admitted that he was badly in need of the money that would come from selling.

"How can you want to sell everything that Mom and Dad worked so hard for?"

"I don't want to—but I might *need* to."

The issue hung heavily in the air between them, whether or not it was actually being discussed. The result was that a half-hearted effort, at best, went into the usual seasonal activities. The meals were simple and the few baked treats that there were had come from the super-market. There were no sleigh rides and no snowball fights, with the pale excuse being that the children were beyond such things and the weather was too cold. The tree was small as well, and the decorations were put up hastily.

The son began to lug the big carton back toward the attic before it was even half empty.

"We didn't hang the mistletoe," the daughter protested, weakly. "It doesn't seem like Christmas without it."

"It doesn't seem like Christmas anyway," the son said. But, because he didn't want to create more tension than there already was, he stopped and rifled through the box until he found the tattered little ornament and gave it to his sister.

She, not wanting to seem as though she was rubbing her sentimental attachments in her brother's face, didn't hang the mistletoe in its usual place in the hall. Instead, she propped it up on a bookshelf where it stood as another sad reminder that Christmas would never again be the same.

On Christmas Eve, the daughter found herself sleep-less. Not wanting to wake her husband as she tossed and turned and worried about the farm, she snuck quietly downstairs for a snack. For more than an hour, she sat in what had been her mother's favorite chair, eating store-bought shortbread and contemplating the future.

She couldn't bear the thought of selling the farmhouse, with all its happy memories. But she understood her brother's very real financial plight. The problem seemed to have no solution, and it had come at a time when she felt ill equipped to deal with it.

"I wish I could talk to you, Mom and Dad," the daughter said, as she stood up and brushed the crumbs off her pyjamas. "Nothing is the same as it used to be."

She started to walk out of the living room, but the mistletoe, slumped sadly on the shelf of the bookcase, caught her eye. With a small smile, she picked up the shabby creation. She hung it from its usual hook in the hallway as she passed by on her way to the staircase.

She had climbed only three steps when she saw the familiar flickering glow.

The daughter caught her breath and silently turned around and looked down the hallway to where she had hung the mistletoe. What she saw took the strength out of her legs. She sank down upon the worn carpet runner and watched in amazement.

This time, there were two lights.

Though equally bright, they were somehow distinct in appearance. Though they swirled together, the daughter could tell where one left off and the other began. For several minutes, the warm, flickering lights illuminated the little entrance hall with their radiant dance. Eventually, the hazy, nebulous shapes met beneath the mistletoe. The flowing forms tightly entwined for several shimmering moments. They grew brighter and brighter until, finally, there was a fireworks-like burst of luminescence that caused the daughter to gasp out loud.

Then the hall went dark again; it was as dark and quiet as if nothing had happened.

But the daughter knew that something had.

As she walked up the stairs and climbed quietly back into bed, she felt a sense of peace and calm within her that had been absent for many months. It was a gift; she knew that. She also knew what to give in return.

Hours later, everyone was awake and the house hummed with Christmas morning activity. The daughter watched for an opportunity to speak privately with her brother away from the chatter and the commotion of the gift opening. She ended up following him into the kitchen when he went to refill his coffee cup.

"Listen," she said. "I've been thinking. I love the farm and I know that you do, too. But the house and the land—those aren't the important things that Mom and Dad built. If I hang on to this property only to watch our family fall apart, I won't have saved anything of value."

"What are you saying?" the son asked, cautiously.

"We'll do what you have to do, even if that means selling. I just wanted to let you know."

She hugged her brother then and returned to the living room. The rest of the gifts were opened, a decent dinner was enjoyed and there were a number of heartfelt eggnog toasts made to Gran and Grandad, who had taught them all of their best holiday traditions.

Two days later, everyone was packing their things and preparing for the drive home. Some were wrapping leftover turkey in tin foil; some were loading suitcases into the cars. The son and daughter were taking down the tree and the decorations, working together in companionable silence. The subject of what to do with the farm had not been discussed since Christmas morning, but both knew that they would be able to work out an agreement.

"About this place," the son said, when they had picked up the last stray strand of tinsel, "there's something...I've had an idea that I'd like to bounce off you."

"Go ahead," said the daughter in an encouraging tone.

"Well—you know I work from home half the time. And there's no reason really that it couldn't be all of the time. And with the kids halfway across the country in college, there's no real need for us to live in the city. So we were thinking—what if we were to sell our house and live here? That would take care of our financial crunch *and* we could hang on to the family farm. We'd pay you rent, you know, for your half—or start making payments to buy you out. Whichever you'd prefer. So—what do you think?"

The son's face was lit with eagerness. The daughter looked at him and smiled.

"I think that's perfect," she said. "But let's forget about the payments, at least for now."

"I want it to be fair," he said.

"Don't worry," she assured him. "It will be. Because we're going to descend upon you every Christmas like a pack of starving dogs, and we'll expect to be shown the time of our lives!"

The son laughed and nodded.

"Agreed!" he said. "That's a deal!"

The daughter reached up then and took the bedraggled mistletoe down from its hook. She handed it to her brother.

"Take care of this then," she said. "I expect to see it next year."

He promised that she would. It was good after all to have that yearly reminder that they had all been blessed with the greatest of gifts: each other.

The Cranberry Glass

Debby was desperately missing her mother on that Christmas Day when David broke the cranberry glass. It had been only a few months since the woman had died and the holidays that year had been full of painful memories. Every familiar ritual came with its own fresh little stab of grief. Every family gathering suffered from the absence of one person. Every ornament that decorated the tree and every special seasonal recipe that was prepared carried with it a sad reminder of her mother. By the time Christmas Day arrived, Debby was as sensitive as an open wound. It was the only excuse she had for behaving so badly.

She was basting the turkey (which contained the apple-prune stuffing that she could never make as well as her mother) when her husband, Andrew, had come downstairs carrying the box that held the six antique goblets that only came out of their foam chips on Christmas Day. They were delicate pieces of hand-blown lead glass in a rosy cranberry shade that matched so well with the holly-and-berries pattern that bordered the holiday china. The goblets were heirlooms; they had belonged to Debby's mother, her grandmother, and her great-grandmother. It was family tradition that they were used only once annually to toast each other and the year ahead.

Andrew set the box on the dining room table and called their teenage daughter away from the television.

"Julianne!" he said. "Set the table for your mother. Dinner's almost ready."

Debby winced and prepared herself for the inevitable argument. Requests made to sound like orders always met with great resistance from their oldest child.

"I'm busy," Julianne whined, predictably. "Why can't David do it for once?"

David was Julianne's five-year-old brother. That less was expected of him in terms of household chores was number one on the girl's top ten list of Totally Unfair Things.

"Sure, I'll do it!" David piped up, scrambling over the back of the sofa and bouncing up the two broad steps that led from the living room to the dining room. "I know how!"

David was seldom concerned about fairness but was eager to take on any chore that put him on par with his sister. His enthusiasm often exceeded his abilities, however, and the image of her clumsy little boy handling her best china and the fragile cranberry goblets sent Debby rushing into the dining room.

"You know what? I'll set the table," she said, hurriedly. "There's a bit of a lull before I have to make the gravy, anyway."

"No," Andrew said, firmly. "You've made the whole supper. Juli's been sitting on her rear end all day."

"Oh, it doesn't matter, really," Debby said.

"It matters."

Andrew's tone of voice told Debby that he wouldn't back down, that he would insist upon having Julianne set the table because there was a point to be made. It seemed that there was always a point to be made where the girl's behavior was concerned, and her father was always willing to be the one to stand firm and make it. Debby, who had to drain the potatoes before they turned to mush, had neither the time nor the energy to negotiate an impasse.

"Juli, please," she pleaded.

The girl tended to be less stubborn with her mother but couldn't be seen to back down entirely.

"David was sitting on his rear end, too," she pouted.

"Fine," Andrew announced. "You'll both set the table, then. Get to work."

Julianne heaved a dramatic sigh and picked up the folded linen tablecloth from the sideboard. She began to shake it out and David clutched at it.

"Let me! I'm helpin'!" he cried.

"Mom!" wailed Julianne. "He's got chocolate on his hands!"

Debby winced when she saw several dark brown smears on the cream-colored cloth.

"David! Wash your hands first!" she ordered. "And Andrew, keep an eye on him, please. Make sure the dishes make it to the table in one piece."

Andrew laughed a little, but it wasn't an overly friendly laugh.

"You're overreacting, Deb," he said. "You should relax and let him try to be useful. At least he *wants* to be." He cast a disapproving look at Julianne and left the room.

Debby went back to the kitchen to drain the potatoes. She stood in front of the sink, in the rising cloud of steam and wished for the 10th time that day that her mother was there. Andrew's condescension, Juli's attitude and David's excessive exuberance had always seemed easier to handle when she had been able to vent her frustrations to a sympathetic ear. Debby's mother had been expert at listening to her daughter's problems, putting them in perspective, and then making her laugh about them.

"Ah, honey," she would always say, "sometimes you have to give 'em one for free."

It had been her way of saying that a person was better off to let go of what grievances they could. It was a good philosophy, and Debby knew that her mother lived by it. Her intrinsically forgiving nature allowed her to let the daily hurts and problems fall away easily. She was left with untroubled affection for each and every member of her extended family. That was why she had always led the round of Christmas-dinner toasts, holding her cranberry goblet high in the air as she said something warm, sincere and special about every person at the table.

Debby mashed the potatoes and stirred the gravy. She took the salad out of the refrigerator and added the oil and vinegar. She buttered the peas and carrots and put them into a serving bowl and checked to see that the wine had properly chilled. She did all of these things while keeping one ear tuned to the activity in the dining room.

Every sound of clinking china caused her to cringe. When she could hear Juli and David quarreling over where to set the salad bowls, she wanted to scream at them to mind what they were doing. At one point, she overheard someone yell "stop shoving!" and pictured some irreplaceable candlestick or centerpiece sailing to the floor and smashing into a thousand pieces.

"Which salt and pepper shakers should I set out?"

Julianne was slouching in the kitchen doorway, looking slightly less put-out than she had earlier.

"The crystal ones, Juli. On the top shelf of the sideboard."

"And where do you want Grandma and Grandpa Baker to sit?"

Debby thought for a moment.

"Far side of the table, I guess. It doesn't really matter."

The girl turned to go, but Debby stopped her.

"Wait a minute," she said. "What's David doing by himself?"

"Well," Julianne drawled. "He couldn't fold the napkins right, and he was dense about how to lay out the silverware, and he's too short to arrange anything in the middle of the table, so I told him to put out the glasses."

Debby's heart stopped.

"The *cranberry goblets?*" she whispered.

Julianne nodded.

"I figured he couldn't screw that up," she explained.

Debby abandoned the cheese tray that she had been preparing and pushed past Juli.

"You know those are precious to me!" she hissed. "How could you have let him handle them?"

She ran down the hallway and into the dining room, where David had just opened the sturdy cardboard box and was lifting up the first of the fragile glasses. He was gripping it by its delicate stem, Debby could see, clearly putting too much pressure on it.

"David!" she said, in a voice that was far more high-pitched and alarming than she had intended it to be. It came out as a shriek and it startled the little boy into jumping. He jumped, and he spun around.

And he dropped the cranberry glass.

There had been plush carpet in the dining room for years and years. The goblet might have stood a chance of survival had it landed on something that soft. Unfortunately, Debby had talked Andrew into replacing the dated, ice-blue saxony with maple hardwood the previous summer.

"It'll look so much better," she had assured him. Of course, she had never pictured it with shards of ruby-colored glass scattered across its gleaming, diamond-hard surface.

Debby felt the blood drain out of her face.

"Oh, my god," she moaned. "Look what you've done!"

David stood uncharacteristically still. Tears had begun to well in his eyes.

"It was an accident," he said, in a small voice. "I didn't mean to."

"No, no, of *course* not," Debby said angrily, as she began to collect pieces of the glass in her cupped hand. "Nobody in this house ever *means* to do anything, but nobody ever *thinks* about what they're doing either!"

Julianne hovered in the doorway, eyeing the situation nervously.

"Mom, I'll clean it up," she said. "Maybe I shouldn't have let David put the glasses out."

Debby turned on her.

"Maybe? *Maybe?* Try 'definitely.' You're always more concerned about yourself—about how you're being treated or catered to—than you are about anyone else in this house, Juli! These glasses have been in my family for generations! Would it have hurt you to keep an eye on them, for me? Would that have been too much to ask?"

Andrew had the misfortune of walking into the dining room then. He saw his two children looking very frightened and very pale, and he saw his wife on her hands and knees, crying, picking up slivers of red glass.

"What's going on?" he asked.

Somehow, the comment put Debby over the edge. She stood up with her handful of broken glass and faced her husband.

"You should have known!" she screamed. "You never consider what's important to me!"

And, with that, she ran out of the dining room, up the stairs and into the bedroom. She slammed the door behind her, sat down on the bed and began to sob uncontrollably.

She cried for the broken goblet and she cried for her children, who would be stinging for days from the horrible things she had said. Most of all, she cried for the woman who had given her the set of cranberry glass, the woman who would never raise her goblet in another Christmas Day toast. Debby cried until she was empty. She cried until her eyes were swollen, and her breaths were coming in hiccuping little bursts, and her nose was plugged solid. Finally, she dropped the broken glass that she had been holding into the wastebasket beside the nightstand and sighed. She pulled a handful of tissue out of the box she kept beside the bed and used it to wipe her blotchy, red face and blow her nose.

"Mom," she said aloud, as she wadded the tissue into a ball and tossed it into the wastebasket, "what am I going to do? I wish you were here. You always knew exactly how to fix things."

And, then, suddenly, Debby found that she was vividly imagining her mother in the room with her. She pictured her sitting at the end of the bed, holding a cup of the hi-test eggnog that she used to make, and laughing her infectious laugh. The image was so colorfully *real* that Debby knew exactly what words would come out of the woman's mouth.

Ah, honey, she would have said. *Sometimes you've gotta give 'em one for free.*

Debby knew that was just what she would have to do. She had to forgive her family for what they had done, and then, perhaps, they would forgive her for the way that she had treated them. She knew that she could do it. The ability to be compassionate was a gift her mother had given her; it was a gift more important than any set of antique glassware.

There was a timid knock at the bedroom door. It opened slightly, and Andrew peered cautiously into the room.

"Deb," he said, in the hushed tone that people use when speaking to those who are dangerously unpredictable, "my parents are here. The food's getting a little cold and..."

"I know," Debby said, and then blew her nose one more time. "I was just on my way down."

Andrew, sensing that he was in no imminent danger, opened the door a little wider and took a tentative step into the room.

"Listen," he said, "I'm really sorry about the glass. I shouldn't have been so pig-headed with Juli and I should have known what would happen if David got close to anything that breakable. I'll try to make it up to you, somehow."

"Thank you," Debby said. "All is forgiven. Now, let's get downstairs so I can make a few apologies of my own."

Ten minutes later, after a round of apologies and hugs, the turkey and trimmings were being busily put out on the table. Julianne was helping, without having been asked. David was being very careful not to touch anything that he wasn't supposed to touch. He was sitting, very still, in the living room, offering his grandparents an excruciatingly detailed description of every gift that Santa Claus had brought him.

When Debby pulled the wine out of the refrigerator, Julianne asked about the remaining cranberry goblets.

"They're still in the box, Mom. Do you want me to put them out, or use ordinary glasses, or..."

"No, put them out," Debby said. "We'll be one short, but that's okay. I'll use a plain wineglass."

Julianne went off to the dining room but returned before Debby had managed to find the corkscrew.

"Mom..."

"What, Juli?"

"I think you should see this."

Debby followed her daughter into the dining room. When she looked at the beautifully set table, she gasped and her hand flew to her mouth.

At every one of the six place settings sat a shining antique goblet made of beautiful cranberry glass.

"I thought there were only six of these, Deb," Andrew said, as he surveyed the festive-looking table.

"There *were* only six," she said. After a moment, she quietly added, "I think Mom just gave me one for free."

It turned out to be a wonderful Christmas dinner, although Debby's mother was greatly missed. Everyone declared that Debby had prepared a perfect meal by herself, though, including the tricky apple-prune stuffing.

"Well, let's see if I can do as good a job of the toasts," Debby said, as she stood up and raised her cranberry goblet.

Later, everyone agreed that she did.

That evening, once the children were asleep and Andrew's parents were gone and the last plate of leftovers had been wrapped in foil and wedged into the overloaded refrigerator, Debby tiptoed upstairs to the bedroom. She sat down on the bed and picked up the wastebasket that sat next to her nightstand.

It contained no slivers of ruby glass. In fact, it held nothing other than the wad of tissue that Debby had earlier thrown away before returning downstairs.

"Thanks, Mom," she said, after several minutes of staring into the nearly empty wastebasket. "Merry Christmas."

She stood up then and started to leave the bedroom. But she paused at the door and looked back at the foot of the bed, where she had imagined her mother sitting hours earlier. Debby found that she was nearly able to conjure the woman's image again and she smiled.

"I'll always remember," she promised, as she turned out the light, "sometimes you have to give 'em one for free."

Part Three: Spirits of the Season

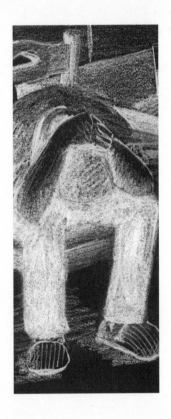

*"Throngs of spirits follow
us everywhere.
We are never alone."*

—*The Ape Man* (1943), directed by
William Beaudine

The Gift Witch

She might have had a real name, but Matthew Burns was
told that everyone called her the "Gift Witch." She lived
out in the country in a poor rural area that was littered
with old trailers and bachelor shacks. In a hovel in the
midst of three debris-strewn acres, she worked her magic.
Though she made herself available year-round, the Gift
Witch was, by far, most in demand in the weeks leading
up to Christmas. Christmas was her busiest season
because, it was said, she could conjure a gift that would
mend a broken marriage.

Matthew went to see the Gift Witch on a cold afternoon in early December. He found her ramshackle house
at the end of a steep, twisting driveway that led down
from the gravel side road that he had followed from the
highway. The place was so decrepit, seedy and run-down
that under ordinary circumstances, he would have
sniffed and turned straight back. The circumstances
weren't ordinary, however—Matthew was fairly certain
that his wife was planning to leave him. Being a man
who did not care to start collecting his own dry cleaning
and hosting his own dinner parties, he was feeling rather
desperate.

Matthew knocked on the makeshift plywood door. It
was opened for him by a nervous-looking, wild-eyed,
middle-aged woman wearing polyester stretch pants and
a lumpy, hand-knit sweater.

"I need to purchase a special gift—for my wife," he
told the witch, as she ushered him into her dingy abode.
"I've heard that you can make very special gifts."

"Oh yeah, sure can, uh-huh," the woman said, as she plucked nervously at her wispy, dark hair. "I make good gifts, yeah."

"I need the kind of gift that will solve my problems," he said slowly, as though he was speaking to a child.

"I know, I know," the witch laughed. "Why else would you be here? Why else would you drive all the way out here in your clean car and your expensive suit? You want to keep your wife, right? Right?"

"It would be extremely inconvenient if she were to leave me," Matthew explained, miserably. "I need a gift that will make her stay."

He handed over an envelope, in which he had placed several folded bills. The Gift Witch took it and opened it. She stopped fidgeting and actually looked quite savvy and capable during the few seconds she spent counting the cash.

"Sure. Oh, sure. Okay," the witch finally said as she tucked the money away in a drawer. "I can do it," she assured Matthew. "I can do the magic, but you gotta get me the ingredients, okay?"

"I suppose so. I mean, it depends what you need," he answered, nervously. He imagined himself hanging around dark alleys searching out a supply of eye of newt.

"Nothing like that!" the witch laughed, as though she had heard his thoughts. "I need things, things, you know, personal things that belong to your wife. Things for the spell."

"Oh, of course," Matthew said, as though he dealt in magic every day and had momentarily forgotten a point of procedure. "Give me a list, then. I'll see to it."

The witch shook her head wildly.

"No, no, no list," she said. "Need three things, but only one thing at a time. Gotta be done slow, slow, real slow and thorough."

Matthew's heart sank. The witch's house was an hour's drive from his office. He'd had to cancel two appointments in order to make *one* trip to see her. He was about to tell her to forget about it, that it wasn't possible. Then he envisioned a life where he had to make his own dinner and buy his own toothpaste and he heard himself saying, "Alright."

"Alright," the witch repeated. "Good. Good, good, good. Now, first thing I need is her scent."

"Her *what*?" asked Matthew, not sure that he had heard correctly.

"Her scent," the witch patiently explained. "The way she smells, like, like, like, perfume, cologne, you know."

"Ah," said Matthew Burns. "Her scent." Then he left the witch's depressing little house, ready to take on his first assignment.

When Matthew got home that night and looked at his wife's dressing table, he was dismayed to find more than a dozen pretty glass bottles scattered across the top of it.

"Do you wear all these?" he asked her in an incredulous voice.

"What do *you* think?" was her defensive answer. Easy conversation between the two had become a distant memory.

"I don't know. That's why I'm asking." Matthew shrugged and put on an expression of innocent curiosity.

His wife shook her head in frustration.

"Well, you should know," she shot at him. "You bought them all for me, for Christmas and birthday gifts. You bought them without bothering to find out what scent it is that I always wear."

She stormed out of the room, leaving Matthew with a problem that was most difficult. It was difficult, but not unsolvable—not to a man who was highly motivated to never do his own laundry.

That night, after dinner, Matthew helped his wife clear the table. In the kitchen, he took advantage of every opportunity to be near her. Then, whenever he was, he inhaled deeply.

"Did you just smell my neck?" she asked him, at one point.

"Smell your...don't be ridiculous," he assured her. But he followed her around for the remainder of the evening, taking deliberate, slow breaths. After a while, Matthew's wife stopped looking at him as though he was crazy. She relaxed a bit and even began to tilt her head this way or shift her body that way to allow him to get just a little closer. It was subtle, of course, but Matthew sensed that she was enjoying the dance, a little. It surprised him to find that he was enjoying it, too.

By the end of the evening, he was well able to select his wife's perfume from all of the bottles on the table. He poured a little of it into a vial and took it out to the Gift Witch.

"That's right. That's good. Good job, then," said the witch, as she put the vial in a dusty ceramic pot, for safe-keeping. She placed the pot on a high shelf, next to several others.

"So what's next, then?" Matthew asked the odd, twitchy woman.

"What's next, what's next, what's next—let's see," she sang. "I know. You buy a bunch of her favorite flowers. Gotta be her favorite; make sure it is. You give the bunch to her, but save three petals. Just three petals; just three. Bring 'em to me."

"Fine," said Matthew. "I can do that." But as he maneuvered his car back up the sharp curves of the skinny driveway, it occurred to him that he hadn't a clue what his wife's favorite flower was.

Roses? No, that was too simple an assumption.

Daisies? They seemed too girlish.

He considered the matter all the way back into the city. Finally, he realized that there would be no guessing his way to success. He had to be sure that he got it right, but he felt that it wouldn't be appropriate to ask his wife directly.

So he phoned her best friend and asked her instead.

"Are you having an affair?" the friend snapped in response to his inquiry.

"What? How did you come up with *that?*" he asked, exasperated.

"You haven't given her flowers in 15 years," the woman said. "You're either feeling guilty or wanting to cover your tracks."

"Look," he begged, "it's innocent, I swear. I want to do something nice and I need you to help me do a proper job of it. Is that so wrong?"

Eventually, Matthew either convinced the friend or wore her down. She gave him the answer that he needed and he stopped at the florist's shop on his way home from the office.

He had never seen such a look of pure shock on his wife's face.

"Lilies!" she said, when Matthew presented her with the bouquet. "I *adore* lilies! Are you having an affair, Matthew?"

"What? No! Can't I just give you a gift without coming under suspicion?" He threw his hands up in frustration.

His wife stared at him appraisingly.

"I suppose you can," she finally said. "It's just a little unexpected. I'm sorry if I seemed ungrateful. They're really very lovely."

She kissed him on the cheek then—something she hadn't done in a very long time—and went off to arrange the flowers in her favorite vase. Matthew went directly to the bedroom, where he wrapped three cream-colored petals carefully in a tissue and placed them in the pocket of his overcoat.

"Excellent, excellent. Very, very, very powerful ingredient," the Gift Witch nodded convulsively as she stuffed the lily petals into the pot with the vial of Matthew's wife's perfume. "This is good, this is good. A very, very, very good start."

"So there's only one more requirement, right? One more item—and then you can make the gift?" Matthew was getting a little nervous about his time line. Christmas was less than three weeks away. If the witch didn't come through, he'd have to send his secretary shopping for a gift for his wife and his secretary tended to get cranky when asked to handle such chores—particularly when the request was made at the last minute.

"One more thing, right, right. One more, one more. But it's big! Oh, yes, yes, yes," said the witch, smiling and fidgeting in her usual crazed fashion.

"Well, tell me," Matthew said impatiently.

The Gift Witch leaned closely into Matthew's personal space. When she spoke, he could smell her foul, vinegary breath.

"You bring me your wife's voice," she whispered.

For a moment, Matthew couldn't think of a single appropriate response.

"Her *voice*," he finally said. "How on earth am I supposed to..."

"Oh, isn't easy, isn't easy. No, no, no. Need a lot of time, to capture a voice. Hours and hours. Days, sometimes. Takes patience. But I'll tell you what to do. I'll tell you; I'll tell you; oh, yes, I'll tell you."

And the Gift Witch did tell him. She told him that he would have to encourage his wife to talk—as much as possible and for as long as possible.

"Make her use her voice; make her tell you things, many things, many things. The longer she talks, the stronger, stronger, stronger the spell. And, while she talks, you carry this in your pocket."

The witch handed Matthew a tiny velvet pouch with a drawstring closure. He looked at it and then looked at the witch, questioningly.

"It's to trap her voice!" she said, as though Matthew was missing the most obvious point in the world. "After all the talking, talking, talking, you pull those strings tight and bring that back to me!"

"Of course," he sighed. "It's to trap her voice."

It seemed to him to be the most ridiculous request of all—as well as the most difficult to fulfill. He and his wife had gotten into the habit of speaking to each other very little, unless they were engaged in an argument. Matthew didn't know if he had the stamina for an hours-long argument so, briefly, he considered giving up the whole crazy idea. But, then, he thought about how horrible it would be to be responsible for sending his own relatives birthday gifts and anniversary cards and he decided that, since he had come so far, he should see the plan through.

"There's nothing to lose, I suppose," he muttered to himself as he crossed the witch's junk-filled yard to his car. "I might as well see if the spell will work."

So he set about thinking of a way to engage his wife in conversation.

"Have you finished the Christmas shopping?" Matthew asked casually as he smeared preserves on a toasted English muffin. It was Saturday morning, so he was enjoying an actual sit-down breakfast. On weekdays, it was his habit to drink a cup of coffee and a glass of orange juice while standing at the kitchen counter perusing the front page of the newspaper.

"What? Why?" his wife said, without looking up from her poached egg.

"Well," Matthew shrugged, "I thought if there were any gifts left to buy that maybe, you know, you and I could do that. Today. Go out shopping."

"Together?" The woman paled and her eyes grew wide, as though she had just received a tremendous shock.

"Yes, together. Of course, together." Matthew heard the irritation in his voice and took a deep breath. "I thought that we could get some lunch, perhaps. Make a day of it," he said, more pleasantly.

He eventually managed to convince his wife that he was serious. The two put on their coats and drove downtown to the fashionable stores that were decorated with tinsel and lights and brimming with other holiday shoppers. The couple browsed and bought, and they discussed the merits of choosing certain gifts for certain people. Matthew casually solicited his wife for her opinions and her advice and after a while, she began to offer both freely.

"I feel as though I'm doing all the talking today," she said at one point.

Matthew smiled and patted the tiny velvet pouch that was in his coat pocket.

"Not at all," he replied.

They stopped for lunch at a romantic bistro that had been their favorite spot for anniversary celebrations when they had still celebrated their anniversaries. They ate salads with arugula and vinaigrette and slivered almonds and shared a bottle of Chablis. After her second glass of wine, Matthew's wife was wearing a mysterious little smile. She appeared to be studying him from across the candlelit table.

"What is it?" he asked. "Did I spill something on myself?"

"No, no," she assured him. "I was just thinking that you seem—different—lately."

"Different good, or different bad?" he asked.

"Oh, relax; it's good. It's quite good," she said.

Matthew smiled then, and he asked his wife another personal question requiring a long, detailed answer. She got to talking, he listened and by the time they left the bistro the stores had all closed, forcing them to postpone the remainder of their shopping until another day.

The following Monday, Matthew delivered the velvet pouch containing his wife's voice to the Gift Witch, who clapped her hands like an excited child.

"Good, good, good. Oh, yes, very powerful, I can tell, I can tell!"

"About the gift, then," he prompted her.

"Not today! Oh, no, not today, no. Takes time to make the magic! In one week, you come back. One week."

She turned her back on him then and took her ceramic pot of ingredients into a back room. Matthew understood that he had been dismissed, so he left. He drove back to the city and waited for seven days.

He was amazed to find that the time passed quickly.

One evening, Matthew went out with his wife so they could finish the Christmas shopping. Another night, she suggested a movie, and although he had carried home a briefcase full of files, he surprised himself by saying yes. Even on the nights when the couple simply stayed home pursuing their separate interests, the hours passed quickly and pleasantly. There was a notable absence of the usual tension that tended to make the time they spent together drag along.

Could it be working already? he wondered one day as he thought about the Christmas gift the witch was making for his wife. There had been some obvious improvements in his marriage. It was reassuring; it kept Matthew from constantly wondering whether he had thrown away both his money and his time.

On the day that he was to pick up the gift, Matthew was more excited than he had been in some time. He arrived at the Gift Witch's decrepit little house before she had even finished her breakfast.

"You wait, just wait. It's ready now, yes it is!" she said in her singsong way, as she wiped oatmeal off her chin and shuffled off into the back room. Matthew could hear her rummaging around; there was the wooden scrape of drawers opening and closing and the dull clink of lids being lifted and replaced on her collection of stoneware vessels. Finally, the witch returned, holding a crudely sewn little sachet in her outstretched hand.

"Here you go!" she said. "Here it is, here it is, here you have it."

Matthew took the sachet from her and examined it. It was nothing more than a few inches of cheap cloth that had been stuffed with cotton batting and doused with perfume.

"*This* is it?" he asked in disbelief. "*This* is the gift that is supposed to keep my wife from leaving me?"

"No, no, no. Well, no, not exactly," the Gift Witch admitted. "It's a charm, you see, a magic charm to help *you* choose the perfect gift, the right gift, the gift she'll love, love, love."

"This is an outrage!" Matthew stormed. "I've made five trips to this God-forsaken place! I've given you hundreds of dollars! This is obviously some sort of con! I don't know how you could have come so highly recommended!"

The witch's eyes narrowed slightly and stopped darting wildly about. She folded her hands together to calm her fidgeting fingers.

"Your friend," she said, in a voice that was suddenly serious and sly, "the one who recommended my services. Is his marriage still together, then? Did his wife stay? Hmmm?"

Matthew paused. He had been told about the Gift Witch, in strict confidence, by his accountant. The man was still very much married, although he was a crashing bore who often smelled like the tinned sardines he liked to eat for lunch. Still, Matthew doubted that his domestic success had anything to do with one of the witch's cheap magic trinkets.

He had been cheated; he was certain of it. But he was equally certain that there was nothing that could be done to remedy the situation.

"What the hell," he said, finally. "Keep the money. Merry Christmas."

He stuffed the talisman into his coat pocket and walked out the door.

"You refill that charm, every month!" the Gift Witch called after him. "Put in new scent, new flower petals, new voice! It stays strong, that way. Strong magic works forever. Forever and ever."

"Amen," Matthew finished bitterly, as he climbed behind the wheel of his car.

Thirty minutes later, as he barreled down the highway, he was still seething. He was angry at his accountant for having recommended such a ridiculous course of action;

he was angry at the Gift Witch for robbing him of his money and making him appear foolish; and he was angry at himself for having been so gullible. His stupidity had cost him a considerable amount of time and money and, worse, Christmas was days away and he still didn't have a gift for his wife.

Although—he did suddenly have an idea for one.

When they had been shopping together, she had insisted on returning to a certain import store several times. There was a folding Moroccan tea table there, a charming piece with a textured brass tray top and mother-of-pearl inlay. Matthew could tell that his wife loved it; he knew that it would make the perfect...

And the witch's words came back to him, then.

It's a charm, you see, a magic charm to help you choose the perfect gift...

Matthew was undone for a moment. He slowed the car and pulled over to the side of the road, where he could stop and think.

He took the sachet out of his coat pocket and examined it very closely. He ran his finger over the loopy stitches that held it together and wondered whether, in her unimpressive way, the strange spasmodic woman with the wild eyes and the wispy hair had performed a bit of real magic.

"Nahhhhh," he finally said to himself. He let out a small, embarrassed laugh and pulled back out onto the highway.

But, still, he returned the charm to the safety of his pocket. Still, he knew that he would refill it monthly, exactly as the Gift Witch had advised.

He reasoned that it never hurt to play it safe. After all, Christmas—and the need for a really good, wife-keeping gift—did return every year.

The Last Good Christmas

It was 3 AM, several frigid degrees below zero and Hank Biddow was outdoors, standing as still as a statue in the black velvet shadows that pooled beneath the overhang of his back porch. Such clear, cold nights were particularly well suited for surveying the view down the gentle hill and beyond the pasture. Besides that, it was Christmas Eve—or technically Christmas morning—a date when a person could do things that were rather out of the ordinary. Not that the retired farmer's behavior was much out of the ordinary. On most nights when he couldn't sleep, Hank would stand on the porch and look down the hill and work himself into a dangerously black mood.

The stars were bright, creating little crystal pinpoints of reflected light in the unbroken crust of snow that had settled on the pasture. It had been two years since Hank had kept livestock, so there were no hooves to trample down the pristine white blanket. So it was all very pretty, very perfect, at least until the eye roamed east past the weathered wooden fence to where Lanny Harcourt's pig barn used to be. The barn had disappeared 18 months earlier, the latest in a depressing series of rural landmarks to be consumed by the creeping suburbia.

Hank could see acres of identical rooftops beginning to take shape where the green and white barn and the yard full of grunting swine had once been. The houses went up so quickly that despite their bright new appearances, Hank suspected a lack of quality. He imagined that within a few short years, the big beige boxy clones with their looming front garages would be looking worn and dull. Not that he would personally witness the decline. Hank knew that the developers would swallow him and his land long before then.

He had known it for years. It had become an inevitability the very day the city had annexed the land.

"It don't mean that they can force us to sell," Hank's wife, Lila, had said.

"In their way, they will," Hank had predicted. "You watch what happens to the taxes, now. Watch what happens to the neighbor farms."

But Lila didn't pay much attention to what went on unless it affected what she was fixing for dinner or the programs she liked to watch on television. She kept to her routines and spent her days comfortably enveloped in the naive faith that everything would be fine, that no one would take away the home that she had been making since she had been a bride.

But Hank was darkly aware. He watched as one neighbor after another sold out to the developers who built one crowded neighborhood after another. He set his mouth in a grim line when there was no one left to rent the grain fields that he was too old to work. And he sold the last of the cows and his one old sorrel mare when he realized that the kids who lived in the cracker boxes had been tormenting the animals by throwing gravel and lumps of dirt at them.

It wasn't long after that the city changed its tax policy.

"This property is within city limits," one particular letter proclaimed. "Therefore, each structure will be taxed as a dwelling." Hank Biddow had the house, the barn, the chicken coop, the equipment shed and the oversized garage and shop, where he had once done his own mechanical work. None of the outbuildings was used for much aside from storage anymore, but when a man had farmed a piece of land for close to half a century, he had a lot of stuff to store. Even the thought of reorganizing his entire world—sorting and selling the old equipment, tearing down the sheds, clearing away the debris—left Hank exhausted. It was overwhelming.

Besides, it felt like time to give up. But in his own way. On his own terms.

Selling would have made the most sense, but Hank wasn't of a mind to do it. So, instead, he ignored the exorbitant tax bill, sat back and waited. He waited and he watched as a pile of neatly typed and increasingly threatening official notices accumulated. Hank tucked each one into the top drawer of his old roll-top desk. It was where he kept all important papers, including letters saying that a person could lose the home that had been his own for nearly as long as he had been a man.

Lila never knew. Hank collected the mail. He had always collected it—and dealt with it. It was just their way. It was her way to go about her day-to-day business carefree and unconcerned and it was his way to stand on the porch with his faded old quilted plaid work shirt thrown over his pyjamas and bathrobe and stare out at the approaching suburbs until his guts churned and his chest felt tight.

Eventually, the cold became too much to bear. Hank turned slowly, like a sentinel reluctant to leave his post unattended, and slipped back through the kitchen door.

The house felt warm and welcoming after he'd stood for so long in the frigid winter air. Hank shrugged off the old quilted plaid shirt and hung it on its usual hook by the door. He took off his boots and placed them neatly on the rubber mat. Then he put on his worn corduroy old-man slippers, shuffled down the hall to the living room and eased into his favorite chair. He switched on the small, green-glass banker's lamp that always sat by his right elbow on the little walnut side table. Across the room, the light bounced off handfuls of tinsel that had been painstakingly draped over the dry, uneven branches of a scrawny pine. The strands shimmered and fluttered like silverfish with every puff of air.

Lila insisted on a tree and made Hank haul out the big box of decorations every Christmas, even though it had been years since their boys—who were actually men living in distant cities—had come home for the holidays. They had their own families to think of and the trip was too far, they explained in the annual apologetic letters. It upset their mother a little each year, but Hank was always quietly relieved. He had raised his kids, done his job with them, but had long ago realized that he and his sons shared no more common ground as adults than they had when the boys had been wailing, round-faced babies. Even during the phone calls that came once or twice a year, Hank never knew what to talk about.

"City's closin' in on us," he had blurted out once, during an uncomfortable long-distance conversation with his oldest son. He had been desperate for something to say.

"You and Mom should sell," the son had replied. "You're lucky the way things have worked out. The land's probably worth a lot more now."

Hank had been appalled. How could his own son, no matter how distant, have such a warped view of their situation? How he could have grown up on the land and not feel its pull?

"Here's your mother," was all Hank had said. He had handed the phone to Lila then, who had just come in from the garden with a plastic pail full of red potatoes and crescents of dirt beneath her stubby fingernails. *Let her talk to the kids*, he had thought. *None of 'em understands a bloody thing.*

It was a thought that came back to him as he sat in his chair awaiting the arrival of Christmas morning. Hank Biddow was certain that no one in his life knew, understood or was even *capable* of understanding the loss that he was about to endure or the indignity that he was about to suffer. He was utterly alone in his worry and his fear. Despite the burden of it, he never entertained the notion of selling.

If he sold, Hank reasoned, they would win. The developers, his boys, even Lila. "If you ain't with me, you're aginst me," Hank's father had often said. Hank believed the old saying and had begun to feel that everyone was against him in some fashion.

The old oak clock with the broken pendulum that hung on the wall opposite Hank's chair read quarter-past three. There were hours to go before Lila got up and started to fuss around in the kitchen. She slept like the dead, aided by some blue capsules prescribed by her doctor. Hank supposed that he could have gotten himself one of those prescriptions but he was reluctant to give up the solitude of the nighttime hours. It was a time when he could think without interruption. There was a work of sorts to be done in the middle of the night. Hank accepted

it; he had taken it on. While Lila worried about nothing and could afford to sleep, Hank had to be awake sometimes.

At first, it had only been "sometimes." Then, slowly, it had become most times. Eventually, during the fall, when the leaves were turning and the crisp, white letters from the city started coming from the legal department instead of the tax department, it had become almost all of the time. Every night, Hank held his solitary vigil and considered his desperate situation.

Despite his increasingly short temper and the redness that wouldn't leave his eyes in the daylight hours, he doubted that Lila even knew. She certainly didn't ask him about it, about how he slept or if he slept. She just prattled on as usual about her canning jars and her bake sales and the people on TV until Hank felt that he might actually slap her. He usually went to the barn when the urge got too strong. Sometimes he walked out on his wife when she was in the middle of a sentence. She never knew that it was for her own good and would treat him with frosty indifference for the rest of the day.

By the time the first snow had fallen, Hank Biddow was sleeping no more than two hours on a good night and had taken to spending every waking minute obsessing about how and when the city would seize the farm. He ate little and talked less. Around the time Lila asked him to haul the cardboard box of Christmas ornaments out of storage, he began seeing things.

That first incident had scared him half to death. It was two o'clock one morning and Hank had been wandering through the silent, semi-dark rooms, as it had become his custom to do. He had been on his way to the kitchen for a glass of water when he saw a stranger standing at the sink.

Hank had actually felt the cold, blue shock of his heart missing a beat. His limbs froze in fear and he gaped at the intruder who was gazing calmly through the kitchen window. Hank's first, wild thought was that someone had broken into his house in order to steal a few minutes' worth of the view. But then his mind came into focus and he realized how ridiculous that would be. When his eyes came into sharper focus, he noticed that the stranger was oddly insubstantial in appearance.

Hank could clearly see the man—he could see that he was tall, with a head of thick, dark hair that stuck up in whorls and tufts. Hank could see the navy blue stripes on his pyjama legs—the intruder had obviously leapt out of bed in order to commit this impulsive break and enter—and the burgundy piping on his silk robe. He could see the stranger very clearly, but he could also see *through* him, to the countertop and the kitchen curtains and even the little ceramic frog in which Lila kept her plastic scrub pads.

"What are you?" Hank rasped when he finally found his voice. "You're not a real man!"

The apparition turned very slowly then, to face Hank. He was darkly unshaven and his face was somehow hollow looking, although he wasn't at all thin. Later, Hank decided that it had been the expression in the ghost's eyes that had given him that impression. In his eyes, when he had looked at Hank Biddow, there had been absolute, stark terror.

The specter's mouth formed a silent "O" of surprise. He regarded Hank for two or three seconds and then vanished. There was no sound, but for a moment, the column of air in front of the old porcelain sink shimmered as though waves of heat were passing through it.

Hank was left feeling weak and unsteady. He grasped the back of a kitchen chair and scraped it noisily across the floor, not caring that it might wake Lila. He sank down upon it and put his head between his knees, the way he had been taught as a boy. It was several minutes before his breathing regulated, his hands steadied and he felt well enough to sit up straight.

When his head had cleared, he immediately began to wonder whether what he had just seen had been a spirit or the hallucination of an overwrought, sleep-deprived mind. He could come to no conclusion. Hank, who usually saved liquor for special occasions, had three stiff shots of brandy before the sun rose that morning.

It occurred to Hank that Christmas morning was a special occasion, one worthy of a drink. In the dining room sideboard where Lila kept her tea towels and her tablecloths and her good silver, Hank kept a bottle of brandy and one of whisky. The whisky was good for a hot toddy when a person had a whopper of a head cold, but brandy was what Hank preferred if he was choosing to have a drink for the sake of a drink. He took the bottle down from its place on the highest shelf and poured two fingers of the smooth amber liquid into a tumbler.

"Merry Christmas," he muttered to himself. He took a short sip of his drink and spent a moment rolling the taste around in his mouth. Then he knocked the rest of the brandy back, poured a considerably more generous measure into his glass and retreated to the living room.

The living room of the farmhouse was the sort of mellow, broken-in, comfortable space that required decades to create. The fabric on the arms of Hank's chair had been worn soft and smooth, despite having been recovered twice. The hardwood floor had been similarly polished by time and use, giving it a pleasant, gleaming patchwork sort of appearance. The pictures on the wall hung somewhat crookedly, but each had been chosen with care. The lamps were mismatched but were perfectly situated for occasions when Hank wanted to read and Lila wanted to do needlework. Opposite the two chairs that the Biddows always occupied, next to the sofa that was used rarely and only by infrequent visitors, there was a television. Lila loved to watch the game shows and the comedies. Old movies appealed to Hank.

Sometimes, when there was a commercial break in whatever program they were watching, Hank and Lila would talk a little. It was not much and it was never about anything important; Hank had long ago accepted that he and his wife had run out of conversation that ran deeper than daily small talk. But they would chat about this or that, things of minor significance. The week before Christmas, however, Lila had broken with tradition. She had tried to talk to Hank about the possibility of selling the farm.

"We can make a good dollar on it right now," she said. "And I think you were right, a long time ago, when you said there'd be no choice eventually."

Hank had been stunned. He was stunned to realize that Lila concerned herself with such things at all, stunned that she could have so badly misinterpreted his words and stunned to hear that she would so easily give up their home. He had shut the conversation down quickly and sharply and had been too upset that night to sleep a single wink.

It was that night that he saw the pyjama-clad apparition for the second time.

Hank had been wandering from one room to another, still fuming over his wife's treasonous suggestion. When two hours of pacing had done nothing to calm him, he thought he would try to sit in his recliner for a while and look for one of the old black and white shows that were used to fill the hours when no one but shift-workers and insomniacs watched TV. Hank walked into the living room and flipped the switch for the overhead lamp. Dim yellow light flooded the room and captured the insubstantial stranger in the center of it.

Hank had driven country roads all his life and was familiar with the sight of an animal that had been startled by the sudden glare of headlights. That was the very look that the ghostly figure wore—it was an expression of fear, shock and confusion intermingled. The apparition turned frantically from side to side, then spun 360 degrees, seemingly trying to get his bearings. Hank watched in amazement. He felt less shock, less fear, than he had on the first occasion. Still, his first encounter with the ghost had taught Hank that he did not want to make eye contact again; he absolutely did not want to see those dark-circled eyes that were filled with pure terror. He had to turn off the light before the semi-transparent man in the rumpled, striped pyjamas caught sight of him.

With a trembling hand, Hank swatted at the switch on the wall. On the third try, he managed to hit his mark. The room grew dark, and when his eyes had adjusted, Hank saw that the phantom stranger had vanished along with the light. Hank had been left alone, leaning on the wall for support, struggling with having just seen the spectral version of someone who looked as trapped and terrified as he himself felt.

In the days that followed, Hank was so distant and miserable that Lila would not have dared to raise the subject of selling out. Not that it mattered; not that it made any difference. She had said it once and once was all it took to tell Hank that she wasn't with him. *She was against him.* Which put her in the majority.

The thought made Hank want to refill his glass. The brandy was creating a warm zone within him and he decided to feed it until it could take the nasty edges off the worries that Hank had grown accustomed to carrying around like the change in his pockets. He got out of his chair with an old-man groan and went over to the sideboard. He refilled his glass and began to shuffle back across the room. Then he paused.

"It's Christmas," he muttered, with a slur that was just beginning to show itself. "The last good Christmas." In Hank's mind, that gave him permission to take the bottle back to his comfortable chair so that he wouldn't be bothered to get up for refills.

But it didn't look enough like Christmas, not with the tree brooding darkly in its corner. Hank thought that turning on the lights would set an appropriately festive tone for someone who wanted to get liquored up before the sun rose, so he pushed the plug into the outlet. Lila's tree came to life and cast a soft rainbow over the ordinarily drab room. Hank let out an uncharacteristic grunt of approval. The brandy was making him sentimental, he guessed, but he liked what he saw. And if a little felt good, a lot would feel better, he reasoned. Hank decided to go for the whole effect and light the Christmas candles too.

Lila had created a number of tacky seasonal decorations from a box of red and green tapered candles and various paraphernalia purchased at her favorite craft store. There were Styrofoam cubes impaled with boughs of stiff, fake greenery and spray-painted acorns. There were bouquets of poinsettia leaves crafted out of starched fabric and red pipe cleaners. There were wads of cotton batting meant to look like drifts of snow. From the center of each masterpiece rose a shiny, wax candle. Several of these works of art lined the mantle, and several others had been arranged on tabletops and bookshelves around the room. Hank supposed that Lila preferred to keep them in a perfect, unused state, for the candles had never been lit. He decided, though, that on Christmas Day—on this last good Christmas—they should be. Hank rummaged around in the drawers of the roll top desk until he found a box of wooden matches and he lit the Christmas candles one by one.

The room was magically transformed. Dozens of flickering little lights, from the candles and the tree, reflected in the polished hardwood and in the glass fronts of the picture frames that littered the walls. Hank Biddow was not a man who easily recognized or appreciated beauty, but he found himself unexpectedly taken by the glowing effect. His mind, trapped for months in an unbroken cycle of fear and depression, temporarily relinquished its burden.

"Ain't that a sight," he breathed as he took a swill of brandy directly from the bottle. For a moment, Hank actually thought that he might go wake Lila and invite her to share the festive light show with him. But then, because he was a little drunk, he set the brandy bottle down a little off-balance, and it fell over on the side table. In his clumsy effort to catch it, Hank knocked the table on its side. The sweet, pungent smell of brandy filled Hank's nostrils as the liquor splashed out over the floor and a rack of newspapers and magazines. One of the candles—a bright red one set in a nest of cotton angel's hair and gold foil stars—fell to the floor with everything else.

"Dammit! Dammit!" Hank swore as seldom as he drank, but the candle flame had caught the brandy-soaked newspapers and had begun to bloom with alarming speed.

Got to smother it out, he thought frantically, and he nearly fell in his haste to cross the room and fetch the blanket that always lay neatly folded across the curved back of the sofa. His efforts compounded the problem, however, when he whipped the blanket off its perch with such force that the tail end flicked across the mantle and tipped over two more of the candles.

It was then that Hank realized why Lila kept her candles strictly "for show." The candleholders all appeared to be highly flammable.

The stench of burning plastic and glue filled the room. Hank tried to throw the blanket over the fire on the mantle, he tried to pat it out with handfuls of itchy wool, but within seconds the flames had touched the nearby draperies and the faded, cabbage rose wallpaper. The fire licked its way ominously toward the ceiling.

The old house had no smoke detectors, but there was a fire extinguisher buried beneath the kitchen sink among the bottles of lemon-oil polish and bright blue glass cleaner. Hank remembered it and spun around. He might have gotten to it in time, he might have managed to control the hungry fire that was feeding on his dry, tinderbox living room, if it hadn't been for what he saw in the doorway to the hall. He saw the ghost.

It was the same ghost Hank had seen before—he had the same dark, disheveled hair, the same blue striped pyjamas and the same haunted stare. This time, however, the specter wasn't looking at Hank. This time, he was intensely focused upon the blaze that had engulfed the magazine rack and was beginning to catch at Lila's old upholstered chair. The ghost watched with apparent fascination as the flames spread. Then it was Hank's turn to gape as the apparition walked over to the burning chair, calmly sat down in it and closed his eyes.

"What are you doing?" Hank gasped, forgetting for the moment that his visitor wasn't flesh and blood. He made an automatic move toward the fellow but stopped when he realized that he could see the worn fabric-covered buttons that lined the back of the chair through the man's chest.

The ghost opened his eyes. A sort of peaceful resignation had fallen over his usually tortured and turbulent features. He looked across the room at Hank—just as his left pyjama leg caught fire—and he smiled.

Despite his nature, despite the desperate situation, despite everything, Hank smiled back. A calm settled over him then, and he forgot about racing into the kitchen to hunt for the fire extinguisher.

Suddenly—despite months of being able to envision only one outcome—Hank knew that there was another way to end things.

He went to the old roll-top desk and opened the drawer that held all the tax notices and all the letters from the city. He pulled them out—a thick, creamy white bundle of paper the size of a brick—and picked up another candle from the little half-moon table that held the telephone. With great deliberation, he touched the flame to the paper. Once it had caught, he tossed the candle carelessly into the corner.

Hank held the burning letters until they began to blister his hand and then set them strategically below the lowest branches of the Christmas tree. When the branches started to crackle and smoke, he shuffled over to his recliner, a corner of which had begun to smolder. He sat down and made himself comfortable.

One of his last thoughts was of Lila, but he assured himself that in her deep, drugged sleep, she would not suffer. He was always the one who had suffered over things, suffered with the burden of knowing terrible things.

"But not for much longer," Hank Biddow murmured as he closed his eyes.

Same as always, as Peter jolted into consciousness, he could still feel the heat blistering his skin. Same as always, he was astonished to discover that his flesh was actually cool to the touch and that he was in the plush, king-sized bed that he shared with his wife and not in the tacky old upholstered chair that was his funeral pyre in the dream.

He always thought of it as a dream, not a nightmare, despite its terrible nature. It was a matter of perspective, he supposed. Peter had a lot of worries; he had a lot of waking nightmares. Being burned alive didn't even come close to making the top of the list.

"What is it?" His wife asked him in her sleep-slurred voice. She hadn't bothered to sit up or even open her eyes.

"Nothing," said Peter. He ran his hands through his unruly, dark hair and crawled out from under the covers. He picked up the burgundy silk robe that he had thrown across the vanity chair a few hours earlier and put it on. "Nothing. Go back to sleep."

He never told her about the things that bothered him and she never pressured him to open up. It was their long-standing, silent agreement, an agreement that Peter definitely felt was for the best. If he told his wife about the things that woke him in the middle of the night, he might eventually break down and tell her other things. Like the fact that his commissions had been down for 15 straight months and the savings account had run dry. Like the fact that he had missed the last two mortgage payments. Like the fact that their various credit cards were all bulging with debt that they couldn't hope to pay off. Like the fact that his grip on the real world was becoming increasingly tenuous. Peter sure didn't want to tell his wife that. Instead, he put on his robe and closed the bedroom door behind him and padded down the carpeted stairs to face another sleepless night.

It was Christmas Eve, and even in the shadows, the living room looked festive. There was a tastefully decorated tree and a miniature Victorian village set out upon the oak mantle. Boughs of greenery adorned with ribbons decorated the archway that led to the hall and, in the art niches and on the bookshelves, the carefully selected, tasteful, everyday sculptures and figurines had been replaced with carefully selected, tasteful, Christmas sculptures and figurines. There were gifts, too—works of art in themselves, wrapped in foil and ribbon and papers so beautiful that it seemed unbelievable that their only purpose was to hide what was within. They had been piled beneath the tree until there was no more room there. The extras were stacked next to the fireplace.

Usually, Peter objected to his wife's holiday excess. This year, he had not. *Let her enjoy it*, he had thought. *Let her and the kids have one last good Christmas.* He just didn't have the heart to bring down such bad financial news during the holidays. He didn't have the energy for it, either. Especially not since he had been sleeping so irregularly.

Peter had been worried for a year. He had been scared since the end of the previous summer. And he had been an insomniac since Halloween. Sleep had abandoned him, bit by bit, until he had begun to feel like a brittle shell of a person, going through the motions of each day. But worse than the days were the nights—filled with lonely, quiet hours during which Peter questioned his sanity.

There were times when sitting in the darkness, he sensed strongly that he was not alone. There were other, more frightening times when he became momentarily disoriented and thought that he was somewhere else—in a house that was dingy and time-worn and cramped and nothing at all like the sleek, modern split-level on which the bank was threatening to foreclose. Those experiences left his palms sweaty and his heart pounding in his ears. Worse, they left Peter wondering whether his sanity had departed along with his sleep.

Or, whether he was haunted.

He had begun his wondering one sleepless night a couple of weeks before Christmas as he had been standing at the kitchen window looking out over the acres of suburban rooftops. It was something he often did. His house was one of a few that had been built on a little rise in the land, something to do with an elevation of bedrock that the developer had been unable to grade even. The result was that, unlike most of his neighbors, Peter had a view. On that particular night, he had seen that view change before his eyes.

One moment, there had been rooftops and smoothly paved streets and manicured lawns. The next, there had been nothing but a vast, snowy field dotted with stands of bare-branched trees. The landscape had darkened as the streetlights vanished. The changed scenery was lit only by pale moonlight, filtered through an overcast sky. As Peter stared, unbelieving, he felt his face go as gray and pale as the clouds.

It took a few seconds for him to realize that more than the view had changed. The window was different, too. The sliding panes in their aluminum frames were gone. The Venetian blind and the plant ledge with its little painted pots of basil and parsley had vanished. Instead, there was thick, warped glass bordered by panels of yellowing eyelet lace. Beneath it, the Italian tile back splash had been replaced by faded Formica and the marble sink had turned into a chipped ceramic basin with worn, old-fashioned stainless steel fixtures. A bug-eyed ceramic frog sat next to the old sink, holding an unraveling plastic scrub pad in its gaping mouth.

Peter had been reeling with shock, trying to convince himself that he was dreaming, when he heard the voice behind him.

"You're not a real man!"

The words were choked and gravelly. Peter's first thought had been that the voice had come from inside his head. But then he had turned to look behind him. That was the first time he had seen the ghost.

It was an old man he saw standing there. A grey, grizzled, somewhat transparent old man in corduroy slippers and a faded plaid robe. He was gaping at Peter, and his red, watery eyes were wide with terror. There was a frozen moment of Peter and the old man staring at one another in mutual fear. Then the ghost simply vanished, the room returned to normal and Peter was left leaning heavily against the counter because his limbs felt like cooked noodles.

After that, the ghost was simply in the house. Peter knew it; he could feel the old man's sour breath raising hairs on the back of his neck. He sensed him in the shadows and caught fleeting glimpses of him rounding corners or slipping through doorways. More than once, he recognized his stricken, fearful expression in the mirror. He dreamed about the apparition, too, on the rare occasions when he slept.

The dreams were always the same: there was a fire, a rapidly growing fire, and the old man was struggling to put it out. Peter wanted to help, but he felt somehow incapable, insubstantial. And the spreading flames were mesmerizing. As Peter watched the fire twist and curl and feed greedily on its surroundings, he realized that he didn't want to make it stop. There was something attractive about it. Something certain. And, so, with a feeling of peace that he only ever experienced in his dreams anymore, Peter sat down in an overstuffed chair that had begun to burn. There was some pain when the fire began to lick at his leg but mostly there was overwhelming relief. Peter always suffered a moment of disappointment upon awakening.

How depressing, Peter thought, as he settled into his favorite chair in the living room. *It takes a nightmare to give me peace.*

It was true, though. In the dream, Peter could feel the flames consuming the sickening worry and fear that had been consuming him. He had found a way out; he had found a way to quit before he failed. For Peter, who had fought the good fight all his life, it was surprising to learn that giving up could feel so good.

That was something worth thinking about.

Peter lifted his tired body out of the living room chair and walked down the broad, dimly lit hall to the kitchen. The digital clock on the microwave read 3 AM, which meant there were hours to go before the kids would wake his wife, eager to run downstairs and tear the expensive paper off of their expensive gifts. There were hours to go and, although Peter didn't think of himself as a serious drinker, he knew how to fill the time.

The cupboard above the refrigerator was filled with an assortment of bottles. Peter rummaged around until he found the one that he was looking for, then pulled it out and carried it over to the kitchen table. He sank into one of the chairs, and while experiencing the odd but familiar sensation that he was not quite alone, he broke the seal on some very expensive scotch that had been purchased for consumption later in the day. Peter thought he might drink the whole thing before breakfast.

It was a very special occasion, after all. It was to be the last good Christmas.

The Field Angel

At first they thought Eric might die.

It was touch and go for a while, the doctor said. The nurses had both nodded solemnly and agreed; it was a tricky business getting a person's body temperature regulated when he had been out in the cold that long. The boy's parents insisted that it *hadn't* been that long, that they had gone looking for him within 10 minutes of his leaving the house, but the medical staff knew severe frostbite when they saw it, even if it was oddly concentrated in blooming stars on his small palms. Even after everyone was able to stop worrying about whether Eric would survive, there was great concern about that blackened flesh on his hands, which had to have been burrowed deeply in the frozen snow. Eventually—and this was in the city hospital, where they could perform greater miracles—it was determined that Eric would be fortunate enough to keep both hands and all 10 fingers.

There were nearly 10 days of worry over Eric's physical condition. At the end of it, his parents expected to feel a rush of relief. Instead, they realized that the time had come for them to find out why their eight-year-old son had wandered out into a field to die on Christmas Day.

So they asked him. And he said that he had been following the Field Angel.

The next day, a new doctor came to visit Eric.

"You know, I have a little boy about your age," the doctor said as he settled himself comfortably in the chair that always sat next to Eric's hospital bed. "His name is Jason."

Eric looked up from his comic book with interest.

"Does he like Spiderman or Batman best?" he asked.

The doctor put on a thoughtful expression.

"You know, I'm not sure," he answered. "I'll have to ask him." Then, having broken the ice, he asked his first question of Eric. "Who's your favorite?"

"Spiderman, I guess," said Eric. "He's got good super powers."

"Do you ever wish that you had super powers?"

"Sometimes, sure. Why not?"

The doctor made a small note on his clipboard without breaking eye contact with his young patient.

"And what would you do," he asked, "if you had them?"

This made Eric pause. He turned to look out the window at the gray parking lot that had been his view for nearly two weeks.

"Not sure," he finally said. "I'd try to help people, I guess."

"And who do you most want to help in this world, Eric?"

That answer came quickly.

"The Field Angel."

"The 'Field Angel.' " The doctor sat silent and serious for a moment, as though he was taking the time to carefully weigh and file the name. "And who is the 'Field Angel'?" he asked after a moment. His voice was smooth, but his pen had begun to scribble furiously.

"This lady. Well, a girl. Like a high-schooler," Eric explained. "She lives in one of our fields. The one beside our house."

"The one you wandered into on Christmas Day."

"Right."

"Right."

There was a lull while the doctor waited for Eric to volunteer more information.

"So—why does the Field Angel need your help?" he finally had to ask.

Eric sighed heavily.

"Well, she's lonely," he said. "She doesn't have any friends except me. And she's stuck in the field. She can't go out of it, not even to come in our yard. And she gets really sad." Eric looked down at his bandaged fingers, which he had been using to tick off the problems on the list. "I guess that's about it," he concluded.

"And what about you?" asked the doctor. "Do you ever get lonely or sad?"

"Not too much," Eric said.

The doctor had to leave soon after, but he told Eric that he would be back to see him again.

True to his word, the doctor visited Eric the next day and the next and the next. He became regular company for the boy and the two grew comfortable being together.

One afternoon, while the January sunshine slanted through the windows and fell in warm, square patterns on the floor, Eric and the doctor talked about their favorite toys.

"I have a thing for practicing my golf putt," said the doctor. "Whenever I sink a putt—which is rare, mind you—there's this recorded voice that tells me 'Well done!' "

Eric laughed.

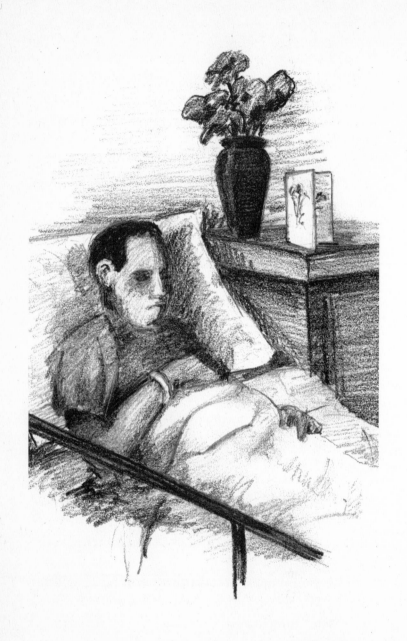

"My mom has a thing in the fridge that makes oinking sounds whenever she opens the door," he said.

It was the doctor's turn to chuckle then.

"Well, I suppose that's also meant to be motivational in a way. But what about your toys? What sorts of things do you enjoy playing with?"

"Computer games," Eric said. "Electronic stuff, like robots. Race cars. I got a radio-controlled monster truck for Christmas."

"Really!" said the doctor. He sounded immensely pleased about the truck. In fact, he was immensely pleased that the subject of Christmas Day had presented itself without any prodding.

"Yeah. It's a really good present. Really fun. I wish I could have it here to play with."

"Are you getting bored?" the doctor asked, although he knew the answer. Every day, the boy seemed more restless. Over the course of 15 minutes, he had moved back and forth between the bed and the window 5 times.

"Pretty bored, I guess. I miss my friends from school," Eric said.

"And what about your friends from home?"

"All the guys I know live in town or else pretty far down the highway. So we just hang out at school."

"So, I guess you might feel bored at home sometimes, too."

"Sometimes."

"Do you ever use your imagination to pretend that someone's there with you? Someone to play with?"

Eric wrinkled his nose and laughed.

"No," he said. "That's lame."

The doctor smiled and shrugged.

"Actually, it's very common," he said. "Very normal."

"Yeah, for lame-os."

"Alright then, let me ask you something else. Do you remember if you were feeling bored or angry or unhappy on Christmas Day?" The doctor spoke casually, but his pen was poised to make note of Eric's answer.

"I don't think so," Eric's voice was quiet. He had moved back to the window and was staring out over the lines of neatly parked cars. "But I don't remember too much."

"You remember getting your monster truck," the doctor prompted.

"Yeah." Eric smiled.

"And you remember the Field Angel."

"Yeah." The smile left the boy's face.

"You remember that she felt sad and lonely."

Eric nodded.

"Do you remember why she wanted you to go out in the field without your coat on?"

"The reason I didn't have my coat on was because I just went outside for a minute, to give my dogs some turkey scraps from Christmas dinner."

"But you stayed outside because you saw the Field Angel..."

"Right."

"And she coaxed you out into the snow."

Eric paused at that. Though he didn't have an adult's command of language, he knew when a word didn't sound right.

"Not 'coaxed,' " he said. "She never made me."

"Then why did you go?"

Eric shook his head. His answers were coming more slowly and his eyes had been downcast for several minutes.

"I just wanted to help her."

The doctor could see that Eric was good for only one more question. He decided to make it one that he had been wanting to ask for some time.

"So you weren't trying to get away from anything? You didn't mean to hurt yourself?"

Eric lay down on the bed.

"No. I think it was just a bad accident," he said before he closed his eyes.

By the end of January, there was no longer any physical reason for Eric to remain in the hospital. The doctor and the parents still held concerns, however, and it was agreed that Eric would be driven into the city once a week so that he could continue his therapy.

Eric returned to school, the winter snow melted away, spring arrived and, through it all, the doctor saw the boy every Thursday afternoon at three o'clock. Sometimes, they discussed what had happened on Christmas Day. Most times, they discussed other subjects, ranging from basketball to the third grade. Eric always seemed very well adjusted, which was disorienting to the doctor, as he was trying to diagnose him.

"So, have you seen the Field Angel since Christmas?"

It was a sweltering day in late May, and the air conditioning was on the fritz. The doctor had his suit jacket and tie hanging on the back of his office door and his sleeves rolled up to his elbows. Eric was sprawled in his usual chair, with his limbs dangling in search of a breeze. Both were relaxed. The doctor had sensed that it was a good time to ask a risky question.

Eric scratched his nose, where the doctor could see three freckles and a rosy hint of sunburn.

"Couple times, since spring" he said. "I didn't get to go outside much before that."

"Has she said anything to you?"

"Yeah, she explained a lot of stuff. She said she's sorry about the accident. She feels bad."

"And why is that?"

"Because she was borrowing my energy when it happened."

The doctor sat up a little straighter.

"Borrowing your...I don't understand," he said.

"Well," said Eric, "it's hard to explain." The boy leaned forward, resting his elbows on his knees. He laced his fingers together beneath his small chin. "She's been there for a long time, in the field, 'cause she was scared to leave. But every year she gets a little weaker, like a battery that's wearing out. So, now she's not strong enough to go away, even though she wants to."

"But she can use your energy?"

"She could use anybody's energy. But I'm the only one who talks to her. I'm the only one she could ask."

"And if you don't help her?"

A shadow passed over the boy's face.

"Dunno," he said. "I guess she'll fade away."

It was the longest speech Eric had ever given concerning the Field Angel. The doctor was so fascinated, he forgot to make his usual note on the clipboard.

Snow fell before Halloween that year. The roads were sometimes treacherous and Eric missed two appointments in a row because his mother deemed it too risky to make the 45-minute drive into the city. When the doctor finally did see him, on a particularly gloomy November day, he noted that the boy was looking different somehow.

"I'm nine now," Eric answered proudly when the doctor made mention of the change.

"Of course, that's it," the doctor said. "Happy belated birthday, Eric!"

"Thanks."

"Tell me, what do you like best about being nine?"

The doctor expected to hear about birthday presents received, new privileges granted or newfound respect from younger friends. He was surprised by Eric's answer.

"I like being bigger and having more energy!"

"I suppose you are bigger," the doctor said.

"Sure I am!" Eric practically crowed. "Nine is way bigger than eight! I know, because I've outgrown some of my clothes from last year."

"And that's been the *best* thing about this birthday?"

"Well, it's the most important thing. This Christmas, I'll have a whole extra year's worth of energy. I'm pretty sure I'll be able to help the Field Angel leave."

The doctor leaned forward. His casual expression had vanished.

"Eric," he said, "you wouldn't go out in the field again this Christmas, would you? Not after what happened last year?"

Eric's happy expression also began to fade.

"But I'm a whole year bigger," he explained.

"Still, you need to think about this very seriously," urged the doctor. "You almost died last year because you were out in the cold for a long time."

"I'll wear my coat this time," Eric said quietly. He was looking out the window, no longer meeting the doctor's gaze.

"Eric..."

"This is her last chance!" The words flew out of Eric in a desperate rush. He never raised his voice, especially to an adult, and he and the doctor both spent the moment that followed in startled silence. "She's hardly even there anymore," he explained, in his usual soft tone. "I can hardly see her; she won't last another year. She's gonna blink out, like a burned-out light."

"And then what would happen to you?" the doctor asked, quietly.

Eric shook his head in frustration. His cheeks were flushed and he turned back toward the window.

"It's not about me," he finally said.

Have completed more than 10 months of therapy with Eric, the doctor wrote in his journal in early December. *This boy maintains a convincing appearance of normalcy yet has shown no signs of abandoning his fantastic story. Even now, am not sure whether patient is genuinely delusional or has woven a complicated fantasy to avoid repercussions for careless behavior. Either way—Christmas Day is obv. significant date which is cause for concern. I feel it necessary to challenge patient's beliefs now as there is risk he may harm*

himself while acting on delusions or attempting to maintain
appearances. Wish there was the luxury of more time. Would
pref. to know which situation I am dealing with.

"I think we ought to talk about the Field Angel, Eric."

"Why?"

There was a guarded look in the boy's eyes that the
doctor had not seen for months. It told the doctor how
much good work had been undone in their last session
and made him wish that the deadline of December 25 was
not staring them in the face.

"Because Christmas is coming," the doctor said,
"which means that it's been almost a year since your accident. It's an important time—a good time for you to start
thinking about what really happened."

"You know what happened," Eric said. He eyed the
doctor suspiciously.

"I know what you told me," the doctor spoke carefully,
"but I think even you know that's not what really happened."

"It *is!* You said you believed me!"

"I believe that it seems real to you on some level. You
have a wonderful imagination, Eric, and it's not uncom-
mon for children your age to create…companions…in
times of need. Maybe to keep them from being lonely. Or
maybe to provide an excuse for guilt-inducing behavior…"

"Why are you talking like that?!" Eric stood up. His
ears had flushed crimson. His hands were clenched into
tight fists.

The doctor rubbed at his temples. *Why am I talking*
like that? he wondered. For nearly a year, he had spoken to
Eric without ever talking down to him. Now, when he

really needed the boy to hear him, he was reverting to psycho-babble.

"Listen, Eric," he said, in something far more sincere than his doctor voice. "Last Christmas, you had a bad accident. It was terrible; it caused a lot of trouble and a lot of worry, but no one blames you for it. No matter what happened—even if it *was* your fault, or if you used bad judgment—no one's mad at you. You should have told your mom and dad where you were going, yes. You should have known better than to wander off to play in the field without your coat and gloves, yes. But you know that now. You learned the hard way. And it's over! There's no need to do it all again this year just to prove you believe in this imaginary ghost..."

"Don't you call her that! She doesn't like that word! Don't say that!"

Eric advanced so quickly that the doctor instinctively threw his arms in front of his face for protection. It proved unnecessary. The boy didn't touch the doctor. He didn't hit or shove or slap. Instead, when he was mere inches away from the doctor's face, he spoke one final sentence that fell like a physical blow.

"I don't want to talk to you anymore."

Eric turned away and left the office. He spent the last 30 minutes of his session sitting on a concrete bench in the chill December air, waiting for his mother to collect him. The doctor stood by his window, just out of the boy's sight, watching over him the whole time.

The doctor and the parents had a brief meeting one day while Eric was in school. It was agreed that Eric would be monitored very carefully on Christmas Eve and Christmas Day. Then it was decided that, no matter what happened, the boy should see the doctor as soon after Christmas as was convenient for everyone involved. The doctor generally did not see patients during the holidays, but he made an exception and an appointment for December 28. He looked forward to the day, knowing that by then Eric would be forced to see things in a different light.

The office was empty and quiet on December 28. Eric was the only patient the doctor was expecting to see, but he arrived early for the appointment, taking the rare opportunity to catch up on paperwork uninterrupted. The time passed quickly and the doctor was surprised when he looked up from his work to see a woman standing in the doorway. It was Eric's mother.

Eric did not appear to be with her.

"Is everything alright?" the doctor asked before he even said hello. Usually, it was the woman's habit to drop Eric off at the front door and then wait for him in the parking lot.

"Yes, everything's...Eric's fine. He's at home. I came to see you instead." The woman remained in the doorway as she stammered out her explanation. She looked pale and tired, and her shoulders were stooped beneath her heavy winter coat. After a moment, the doctor remembered his manners and invited her in.

"I'm sorry—have a seat," he apologized. "I was just, well, concerned for a moment, when I saw you instead of Eric. I thought perhaps something had happened."

"Something did happen," the woman said. "That's why I came. I wanted to tell you about it."

"Alright." The doctor sat down in the chair opposite Eric's mother and waited for her story.

It was awhile in coming. The woman first spent several minutes simply staring at her gloved hands, which were folded primly in her lap. Then she took a deep breath and shook her head.

"I don't know how to tell you so you'll believe me," she finally said, "so I'll just tell you. Eric wasn't making up stories. The Field Angel is real."

"In what sense?" the doctor asked. He wished that he had pushed the record button on his tape recorder before sitting down.

"In what sense? In the *real* sense. In the sense that Eric's not lying and he's not crazy—despite the fact that those were about the only two options we could see."

"Eric can be very convincing..."

"He didn't convince me. I'm ashamed to say I never once believed him. Not until three days ago. Then I saw the Field Angel for myself. Seeing is believing, right?"

"The eyes can play tricks..."

"Not this time," the woman snapped. "If I had seen her from the house, maybe. If I had caught a fleeting glimpse, maybe. But that's not the way it happened."

"How did it happen?"

"Like this," said the woman. "Eric was miserable all day long. I didn't think it was possible for a kid to be so purely miserable opening his Christmas presents. We spent the whole day trying to make him happy, but nothing worked. All he wanted to do was go outside to look for the Field Angel. By himself, mind you. But we wouldn't let him. Like we talked about before, it just seemed too much of a risk. But by after supper, he was moping so bad, I finally said, 'Okay, you can go. But I'm going to watch you from the tree line.' He wasn't too thrilled with that, but he knew it was the best deal he was going to get.

"So we put on our coats and boots. I told my husband to wait inside; I said we'd only be a minute. I wish now that he had come with us, except maybe it wouldn't have happened the same then. Who knows? But we walked out back of the house together and then I waited by the trees while Eric started off into the field. I felt sick, watching him walk out there alone. I could see the trail of footprints he was making in the snow. It looked just like the trail we followed last year when we went looking for him.

"He trudged out about a hundred yards, I guess, and I was just about to call for him to come back. But then he put up his hand, like he was waving to someone. That's when I saw her. She was real faint at first. Just this shimmering kind of lavender-colored shape hovering over the snow. It was like there was a light shining at the center of the shape. As the light got stronger, the features became more distinct."

"Would this have been around sunset?" the doctor interrupted. "On occasion, the setting sun can create reflected images..."

"The sun had already set," the woman stated flatly, "and I know the difference between a reflection and what I saw. Especially since I saw her up close."

"You said you were by the house..."

"At first, yeah. But as soon as I saw this thing, I got scared for Eric. I went running out into the field after him. I was calling his name and he was trying to wave me away. I think he thought that the Field Angel would disappear if I was there. But she didn't. And, as it turned out, it was a good thing I followed Eric."

"Why is that?"

The woman smiled, but not at the doctor.

"Because I'm 40 years old," she said. "Because I'm much larger than a nine-year-old boy and I have more energy to spare."

"You can't be serious!" The doctor was incredulous.

"I am," said the woman. "You would have done it, too, if you had seen her. Sweet little thing and very weak. She needed to go wherever it is we go when we're done here. Eric couldn't help her. He wanted to be the one to do it, but I wouldn't let him. Not after what happened last year. So I held out *my* hands instead, and she held on to them. It felt like someone was running ice water through my palms. Eric and I watched her light get brighter and brighter and then, all of a sudden, she was gone. I was freezing cold then, I can tell you, and I felt about ready to faint. But we both could feel that it had worked—that she had gone to the right place. We knew that my energy got her there."

The woman stopped talking. Her story had ended. The doctor tried to think of something to say but found himself at a loss. He was debating whether his next call would be best placed to Eric's father or some impartial social agency.

"That's okay," the woman sighed, as though she had been monitoring the doctor's thoughts. "I never expected you to believe me without proof. That's why I came to see you instead of calling on the phone."

She stood up then, wearily, and peeled off her gloves. She held her hands out for the doctor's inspection. In the middle of each palm was a blackened star-shaped mark with angry-looking red-and-white tentacles creeping toward the fingers. It looked for all the world like frostbite.

Before the doctor could comment, the woman did.

"I imagine they'll heal up soon enough," she said. "Eric's only took about a month."

Then she turned and left.

The doctor never saw Eric or his parents again, and he never phoned anyone to voice any concerns about the boy's welfare. After a careful review of his notes, he came to believe that the situation had somehow resolved itself.

Though he couldn't quite allow himself to believe what Eric's mother had told him, the story stayed on his mind. And, every once in a while, when the doctor felt lost with a patient and needed to open his mind and think more creatively than usual, he would take a drive in the countryside. At some point, he would pull over to the side of some gravel road and stare off across the prairie until he felt he had an answer.

"Where have you been?" his receptionist would sometimes ask him when he returned.

"Looking for Field Angels," was always his reply.

A Good Prospect

Lewis Bunker had always sold door-to-door. He liked the freedom, he liked the challenge and he was proud of the fact that he had a certain talent for it. Sometimes, before he even knocked on the door of a house, he could tell whether he was likely to make a sale there. His experience and his hunches—which told him where to invest his time and effort—helped him to be terrifically efficient. That was of great value, particularly on the rural routes where he had to spend more time driving and therefore had less time to pitch his wares.

If a place was a bit run down—if there was a mean, skinny dog patrolling the yard and old paint peeling off the window frames—Lewis knew that he wasn't likely to make a dollar there. He wouldn't dismiss the opportunity altogether, but he wouldn't waste too much of his time. If, on the other hand, a farmhouse was tidy and pretty, he knew that his chances of selling something were good. "A good prospect," he would always say to himself as he parked the car and brushed the potato chip crumbs off his lapels.

He was working a new route one overcast day—a long stretch of winding country road dotted with acreages and small farms—when he first saw the Petrie place. It was a very good prospect: a well-kept, freshly painted Victorian house with charming flower boxes that would have been bursting with marigolds and geraniums had it been July instead of early November. Lewis knew from experience that such houses would be magically lit and colorfully decorated come the holiday season. The people who lived in them would send out dozens of pretty cards to their friends and exchange thoughtful gifts, wrapped in glittering papers and topped with splendid bows. This was all most important, because Christmas was what Lewis Bunker sold.

From his brochures, his catalogs and the two huge, boxy sample cases that always sat in the trunk of his second-hand sedan, Lewis sold gift wrap, ornaments and holiday treats. He had tinsel rope in five different colors, when most stores carried only silver and gold. He offered two dozen different lines of boxed greeting cards—ranging from those offering deeply religious sentiments to those wishing people a generic "happy holidays" with some cartoonish Santa Claus or snowman figure. He sold cookies and sweets packaged in tins that were so handsome, they could be given as gifts. He carried snow globes, wreaths, colored lights and spools of shining ribbon. It was a particular challenge, making people plan for Christmas when it was still weeks, or even months, away, but Lewis could do it when he was given a good prospect.

The gate had been left invitingly open, so Lewis steered down the long driveway right into the yard and parked next to the tall, immaculate green-and-white picket fence. He used a shot of breath spray to hide the evidence of his beef-jerky-and-cola lunch, hauled his sample cases out of the trunk, walked up the broad steps of the front porch and rapped lightly on the door.

A smiling, middle-aged matron opened the door before Lewis had even pulled back his hand. He was momentarily startled but then smiled in return and launched into his pitch.

"Merry Christmas, madam," he said, in a smooth, practiced way. "Too early, you say? It's never too early to plan for the holidays, which is what I am here to help you do. I'm Lewis W. Bunker, a representative of 'Christmas Creations,' the only company that..."

"Oh, yes. Come in, please. I'm Marian Petrie."

Lewis usually had to deliver much more of his speech before a customer would be intrigued enough to invite him in. Sometimes he even had to lure them by taking one or two of the flashier items out of his cases. But there was Marian Petrie, already holding the door open wide, smiling brightly and motioning for him to step into her lovely foyer.

"I'll make tea," she announced as Lewis crossed the threshold. "Come into the kitchen and we can visit while the kettle boils."

As he followed his hostess down the gleaming hardwood floor of the hall that led from the foyer into the kitchen, Lewis noted that she looked to be every bit as well-tended as her home. Marian Petrie's silvery hair was set in soft waves that framed her subtly made-up face. Her conservative print housedress had been crisply ironed and the ruffled apron that was tied around her trim waist was snow-white. Lewis, whose ex-wife had worn sweat pants and sneakers even when she went out shopping, was impressed.

"Your home is lovely," he said, as they entered the large, sunny kitchen, with its shining, red-and-white-checkered tile floor.

Marian turned to Lewis and thanked him with her dazzling smile.

"It requires a lot of energy," she admitted, "but I'm so pleased that you find it appealing. Have a seat, Mr. Bunker, and I'll make the tea."

Lewis sat down at a polished oak table next to a large window that overlooked the back yard. The clouds outside had broken, and light streamed through the glass. A pretty sun catcher, dangling in front of the center pane, cast little geometric shapes of colored light over the catalogs that Lewis had begun to spread neatly across the table.

"I'll get that out of your way," Marian said, as she moved a glossy, potted poinsettia from the middle of the table to the far end. Lewis looked at the plant and smiled.

"Getting into the Christmas spirit already, I see! That's terrific. Most people wait until the last few days. They don't get full value from the holidays."

Marian nodded, as she efficiently emptied the kettle into the teapot and arranged shortbread cookies on a delicate china plate.

"Oh, I agree. It's best to make the most of the season. I find it's such a wonderful time of year for visitors. People tend to be more social at Christmas, don't you agree?"

"Yes," said Lewis, who had a policy of agreeing with anything a customer said. "And, if you entertain a whole lot, you might be particularly interested in looking at our 'Special Occasions' line of tableware, centerpieces and ornaments."

"Mr. Bunker," Marian said solemnly as she placed a cup of steaming black tea in front of Lewis, "I am particularly interested in *everything* you have to show me. I'm certain that it's all quite wonderful and that I will find many things I wish to buy."

Lewis could barely keep from rubbing his hands greedily together. He proceeded to cover the oak table with samples of his wares, all the while thinking about the large steak dinner he would buy himself when he got back into town that evening.

Marian spent a great deal of time oohing and ahhing over the glass baubles and tree toppers. She commented on each design of wrapping paper and devoted considerable energy to matching particular patterns of paper with particular shades of satin ribbon. And she listened with great fascination as Lewis went into depth about the virtues of each different Christmas card.

"This specific one's called 'The Scenic Season,' " he explained as he held up one card for Marian Petrie to inspect. "The message inside is kind of brief, but the picture's terrific, I think. Atmospheric. You take a look, you'll see that's really quality artwork."

Marian Petrie took the card out of Lewis' hand and looked closely at it. The front featured a watery pastel painting of a house that was much like her own but beautifully trimmed with Christmas finery. Multicolored lights framed the windows and a large wreath of greenery, tied with a pillowy red velvet ribbon, hung upon the door.

"It's so lovely," she breathed. "I should have thought of that. It just takes such energy. To decorate the house that way, I mean."

"It's easy enough with 'Christmas Creations,' " Lewis said. Then, knowing that it was time to let the merchandise sell itself, he sat back and relaxed while Marian took her time browsing through the catalogs and examining the samples on the table.

Lewis sat quietly and listened to the music of an oldies radio station that was drifting in from another room. He gazed around the kitchen and smiled when he noticed an ancient calendar that had been kept for the sake of its pretty picture. Finally, for the sake of something to do, he took a sip of his untouched tea. It was so awful, he very nearly spat it out again.

The tea had become cloudy and bitter as it had cooled, and it left Lewis with a gritty, muddy aftertaste in his mouth. He took a cookie from the chipped china plate, hoping that a bite of something sweet would solve the problem. Instead, the shortbread crumbled like chalk between his teeth.

Old ladies and their gawdawful dry cookies, Lewis thought to himself. He was often served tea and cookies in his line of work and had learned that the more elderly the hostess, the more likely it was that the baked treats would require dunking.

Of course, Marian Petrie hadn't seemed that old. At least, not when she had first welcomed him into the house. But, as she sat hunched over the catalogs, choosing between foil and iridescent gift wrap, her years were showing. The hair that had looked silvery and soft in the flattering light of the foyer appeared, in the kitchen, to be the color and texture of steel wool. Lewis saw that Marian's rosy complexion was actually quite sallow beneath the blots of rouge and that her skin was speckled with age spots. When she looked up and smiled at Lewis, delighted by some trinket she was holding, he could see brown stains creeping out from between her teeth.

The light must be pretty harsh in here, he thought and instinctively glanced up at the ceiling. Where he had expected to see a handsome fixture, there was a dangling, naked bulb.

"Where are the other gift wrap samples you showed me?" Marian asked. "The fancy ones. The more expensive ones."

Lewis pushed away his petty thoughts and pulled out his other sample case. It didn't matter one bit if Marian Petrie had unruly hair and blotchy skin. All it really took to make people seem attractive to Lewis was that look of *want*, that expression that told him they were going to buy. There was really no such thing as an unattractive good prospect.

"These are real nice," Lewis said, as he leaned over and rummaged through the case on the floor for his textured paper samples. "They do cost a little more, but anything of this quality is bound to...*what the hell!*"

Lewis leapt to his feet, knocking his sample case skidding across the kitchen floor.

"What is it?" Marian asked. "What's wrong?" She looked at Lewis with alarm.

"I'm sorry," he gasped, "it's just a mouse." As his breathing slowed, a red flush of embarrassment began to rise from beneath his shirt collar. "I'm not scared of mice or anything, it just gave me a start," he explained. "It ran over my hand." He compulsively brushed at the back of his left hand, as if trying to rid himself of any remaining traces of the creature.

"Oh, dear. I am sorry," Marian said. "It's an old house, you know. They crawl in through the baseboards all the time."

Lewis frantically scanned the baseboards in search of other skittering intruders. He saw nothing aside from scarred, grimy floor tiles that had begun to curl up at the corners.

And he didn't understand how that could be.

Lewis had noticed the floor when he had first walked into the kitchen. It had appeared polished and perfect then. Now, it was dull and worn through in spots. Some chunks of tile had broken off entirely and peeled away, leaving a rough, filthy patch of dried glue over the wood.

"Mr. Bunker, you don't look well. Can I get you some more tea?"

Lewis sank back into his chair and shook his head. He was feeling oddly disoriented but still had the presence of mind to refuse a second cup of Marian Petrie's horrid tea.

"A cool cloth, then," she pronounced, "to put on your forehead." She scraped her chair back over the ugly floor, stood up and walked briskly out of the room.

Lewis could hear the sound of water being run in some distant room. He could still hear the radio, emitting a tinny version of another old, romantic standard. He thought he heard the stealthy scratching of tiny rodent feet behind the walls. But while his ears took in many things, his eyes could only focus upon one: the back of the chair in which Marian Petrie had been sitting.

It was nearly enshrouded in a thick, gauzy web. A fat, black spider sat at the center of its intricate handiwork, stretching two of its eight long, hairy legs.

Lewis Bunker shuddered with revulsion and forced himself to look away. Averting his eyes was of no use, however, for everything in his field of vision seemed to fill him with confusion and dread. When he looked at the potted poinsettia, at the opposite end of the table, he saw that the healthy leaves had suddenly become black and curled. When he turned to the kitchen window, he saw that it was not the same pleasant window he had glanced through earlier. The glass had turned cloudy with layers of grime, and several of the panes were cracked. The thin light of the overcast day was barely able to penetrate it. Not that it mattered, for the cheery sun catcher had vanished altogether. By the time Marian Petrie returned to the kitchen with the damp cloth, Lewis was hyperventilating and stuffing his samples back into his two large cases.

"Mr. Bunker! Are you alright?" Marian asked.

Lewis risked a glance at the woman and saw that the flesh beneath her cheekbones had sunken deeply. It appeared as though she had lost 15 pounds during her two-minute visit to the bathroom. Her dress had faded as well, and it hung crookedly on her skinny frame. Her previously white apron was the color of dirty dishwater.

"I have to go," Lewis said, when he found his voice. "I just have to leave, please."

"Oh, no! No, I haven't seen everything yet. We haven't really had a chance to talk! I'd love a visit—please stay!" Marian's voice had become different somehow. There was an undertone to it that was guttural and rasping. She took a step toward Lewis and reached out to touch his arm. He watched her bony hand advance; he saw her broken, thick, yellow fingernails come to within inches of his person; and he knew, instantly, how vile her touch would feel.

The look of want was still alive in Marian Petrie's dull, clouded eyes. But, suddenly, Lewis Bunker understood that what she wanted was not in his catalogs or his sample cases.

He recoiled so quickly, he knocked his cup and saucer crashing to the floor.

"Leave me alone," he begged. "Just let me go!"

Marian shook her head.

"But I only want some company," she croaked. "I enjoy a visit so much. It's not easy to do, you know, but I fixed the house up nicely, so you'd want to stop. You looked like such a good prospect."

As she finished speaking, a small bug crawled out of Marian Petrie's mouth and scurried across her slack cheek. Lewis watched in horror as the insect burrowed into his hostess' coarse, colorless hair, and he decided that he didn't need his catalogs and sample cases after all. He ducked past the woman, performing an almost contortionist-like maneuver in order to avoid touching her or brushing against her decaying clothing, and he ran.

Lewis ran down the hallway, where the gleaming hardwood had reverted to dull, worn planks. He ran across the foyer, which had become thickly coated in dust, and he yanked open the splintered, swollen, front door. As he skidded across the porch, which had sunken deeply into the ground at one end, he could hear panes of window glass bursting into shards behind him.

The car was still parked in the same place, but the fence had moved. It was leaning, precariously, threatening to collapse against the grill of Lewis' sedan. The pickets, which had been a cheerful green and white when he had first seen them, were the dim, gray shade of weather-beaten wood. As Lewis leapt into the driver's seat and jammed his key into the ignition, he could hear a loud creaking. He jammed the gearshift into reverse and pushed on the gas pedal. No more than a second after the car lurched backward, the groaning, rotting fence collapsed, sending up a spray of powdery snow.

As Lewis sped down the long driveway, he risked one backward glance. The rearview mirror showed him a house that was disintegrating before his eyes. The color was bleeding out of the siding, the shingles were curling, and the foundation was crumbling. Lewis could hear the tortured scream of stressed wood as the house sank in one corner, tilting several dangerous degrees. Just as he was about to look away, however, a sudden burst of light and color captured his attention. He slowed the car to a crawl and turned to gape at the house. There, enticing him to return, were twinkling lights, framing the broken windows. The weathered front door, hanging loosely from one hinge, was suddenly made festive with a full, green, wreath that was tied at the top with a voluminous red velvet bow. The decorations were identical to those depicted on the Christmas card Marian Petrie had admired.

It just takes such energy...

Lewis could see it then, he could see the image shimmering and flickering before his eyes, as some force struggled to maintain it. It was mesmerizing; he sat and watched, with his jaw hanging stupidly open. Had he been any farther from the road, he might not have heard the metallic scraping sound. But, as it was, Lewis did turn around in time to see the hulking ruin of a gate attempting to drag its leaning self out of the ditch— attempting to close itself and block the driveway that led to the main road.

Lewis nailed the gas pedal. He didn't look back again, not even after he was miles away, safely barreling down the highway that led into the nearest town.

The neighbor who was unfortunate enough to have a full view of the eyesore that was the old Petrie place had been watching as Lewis careened onto the main road and sped away.

"Well, he's finally gone," she told her husband. "Left in an awful hurry, too."

The husband, who was reading his newspaper and had little interest in the doings of his neighbors, living or dead, only grunted.

"What could he have been doing over there, all this time?" the wife wondered aloud.

"Dunno," said the husband.

"He went in that old wreck of a house, too. That can't be safe."

"Hmm," said the husband.

"It's odd; it happens so often," the wife mused. "Marian Petrie's been dead for 20 years and she gets more company than we do."

The husband sighed and folded his newspaper.

"Probably just real estate people," he said. "You watch—the Petrie kids are gonna sell that old place sooner or later. Someone will pick it up and build a new house there."

The wife thought of how nice it would be to have a neighbor to talk to and a view of a lovely, new home instead of a falling-down wreck. She smiled.

"Do you think so?" she asked her husband.

"Sooner or later," he said. "Someone'll snap it up. It's a good piece of property, after all. A very good prospect."

The End